Arsenal

Tammy Swofford

Arsenal

Library of Congress Cataloging-in-Publication Data

Swofford, Tammy,
Arsenal

ISBN -13: 978-0615599243
ISBN – 10: 0615599249

For

Yusuf

Table of Contents

Table of Contents

When the number of Believers reaches three, then this faith tells them, "Now you are a community, a distinct Islamic community, distinct from the jahili society which does not live according to this belief or accept its basic premise." Now the Islamic society has come into existence (actually).

Sayyid Qutb

To Allah We Return

Dr. Muhammad Rahimullah, Ph.D was as thorough a man in death as he had been in life. He had purchased a burial plot in a Muslim cemetery situated within a few kilometers of Beirut, Lebanon where it had been his intention to spend the last years of his life with his wife Khadija.

Along with making his small purchase he had chosen to have the first physical exam in two decades. So it was that he took part of an afternoon to visit with Dr. Ahmed while seeking reassurance regarding future health. Receiving a glowing report from the physician in the ancestral village of his scholarly family, Dr. Rahimullah became psychologically reinforced that he might make the centenarian mark. Granted, his physical involved only a head-to-toe assessment with a gentle little prod of his prostate, a chest x-ray and 12 lead EKG. The clinic also boasted a sonogram machine, but as his digestion was in good order it seemed silly to incur the expense. Looking at his lower legs, no longer populated with hair follicles, the physician quietly proclaimed him to have peripheral vascular disease and made discreet enquiry as to his marital bed. "You know," said Dr. Ahmed, "when the legs have lost their hair up to the knees most men find it impossible to be the bed-owner anymore." Quite startled, Dr. Rahimullah blurted out that he was as strong as Al-Qaswa' the she-camel of Prophet Muhammad (PBUH), with regard to endurance. His wife, Khadija, had little interest at her age. With a smile he added mischievously, "We know that angels are raining curses down on her head."

Dr. Ahmed responded, "Of course then, you will seek out a second wife on your return to Lebanon. But should you need, I have a small homeopathic option used successfully by older men."   The physician swept his hand across a shelf with a caravan of bottles containing dried herbs. Selecting the largest bottle containing a selection of dried leaves and what looked like insect wings he happily proclaimed, "Allah wants us to populate the earth and it matters not the age. It is possible with this tea. I tell you with all confidence that I am quite active myself, albeit my wife's interest is no greater than the size of a date seed now. Not suitable for anything. But with a second wife...." His voice trailed off and Dr. Rahimullah uttered a hopeful "Insh'allah" and nervously moved the conversation to a new topic.

Dr. Rahimullah planned on returning to the United States to spend a final year passing his duties on to his colleagues. He looked forward to the next season of his life. He would close his eyes and fix a mental image. He was seated on a small bench outside his village home with a stack of books. Khadija served tea as his bones soaked in the heat of the afternoon sun. He would watch the advancing evening shadows. There was a grapevine near the wooden bench by the back door and the small fruit orchard to the side of the house would provide the scent of creation. Several years prior Dr. Rahimullah had also purchased two small burial plots in a Muslim cemetery on the outskirts of Deerborn, Michigan. He now had full intention to leave the plots to his adult sons. On his return to Lebanon he would seek out a pious widow in a nearby village who was poor enough that her family would accept a small dowry, and enjoy again what he now began to sorely miss in his life. In his mind, he played out his Friday prayers followed by a bit of time spent with his second wife.

Khadija, long past caring, was perplexed by the sudden burst of energy from her husband on his return from the doctor. Thinking him happy with the thought of returning to a more simple way of life she spent her days visiting the relatives and going through a re-familiarization process of the local open air market. Little had changed yet somehow everything had changed. The wooden stalls with the acrid smells of animal stench mixed with grilled kebabs took up residence again within her sensory memory. But the faces had changed. The former merchants now sat dozing on the cement steps of their homes and their children ran the stalls. Feeling a bit old, Khadija fortified herself a bit to bustle along with a bit more speed. But it was hard to pull off the look of invigorated youth because of her voice. It rang out loudly in greeting, as is the manner of those who are going deaf but not yet aware of the decibel adaptation to deal with the sensory loss.

Dr. Rahimullah was quite practical regarding aging. He had always believed what his grandfather shared with him as a small child. Allah had made the pen first and told it to write the destiny of mankind. Before creation, before the clot of blood, his fate was sealed. The pen had written the final chapter of Dr. Rahimullah's earthly life long before it ever began. The day of ensoulment was also the march toward physical death. As a Sufi he did not fear death. But what was stitched into his soul was a desire to return to his roots and to be placed in the ground in a Muslim cemetery quite near his place of birth.

We make choices throughout life. One major choice is made for us by another. It is the moment of our demise. Khadija found her husband lying dead atop the prayer rug in his study three days after the return to Michigan. Death took him by surprise. His little bottle of herbs was on his desk and a copy of his EKG was still folded neatly into his wallet.

Now while it is desirable to die at the time of Sajdah, Dr. Muhammad Rahimullah missed out on his other three interlocking goals: to die in a masjid, during Ramadan, and better yet, on Lailatul Qadr itself. But fate did not grant his flight of fancy. When Khadija had initially peeked into the study she didn't note the odd placement of his hands. Hobbling along on her bad knees she feigned an illness to skip the Fajr prayer. In actuality, the final leg of the flight had left her cramped into a small middle seat with her husband sleeping with his small pillow cushioned by the window and the aisle seat with a German teenage boy who smelled like alcohol. The "illness" was sleep deprivation. She could no longer handle the long flights, time zone changes, and the hassle of moving through customs.

Making her way into the kitchen, she contemplated cooking a small breakfast. Thirty minutes later she returned and noted the waxy appearance of death in the features of her husband. Reaching for a phone on the desk she dialed the eldest son. "Shaheed! Isra'il has taken your father. Notify Yusuf!" And with that, she returned to the study to seat herself beside her husband. She had no idea what to do next.

The area medical examiner signed off on the death immediately when contacted by the neighborhood imam. The body was washed and shrouded in short order and the news of Dr. Rahimullah's demise was sent out in a communications blast to his closest earthly associates.

Wrapped in his karfan with the imam of the masjid standing at the front of his head ready to deliver the funeral prayer, Dr. Muhammad Rahimullah was a man whose name was recognized by thousands. He was a Da'iyah. But his instructions regarding his funeral and burial had been very specific. Very few men were to be present, and the men listed on the hand-scrawled note were few in number.

When all was said and done Dr. Rahimullah was placed into the ground with very little fanfare. His wife took the allowable three days for grieving. Afterward, she moved in with her eldest son and daughter-in-law to observe Iddah. The house was closed up and a man was hired to manage the lawn. The widow's season of waiting ensued. A younger widow might hope for a marriage proposal during the waiting period. Khadija knew that such a prospect was unlikely. Her husband had been a formidable and pious man. She had been his faithful wife. Few were the men in number who would consider approaching her son with a proposal of marriage. She reflected that to pious men belonged the pious women. It was as Allah willed. The pen had written her destiny. She had married a powerful and well-connected man. Although not educated beyond a high school level, she had continued her education at home. She had read many of the books which lined the shelves of the office. Her sons had been taught to read the Qur'an while seated on her lap. They had married pious women and produced grandchildren. The generations were strong. She had done her part. She would take her memory and build a fortress against her grief. She allowed her mind to drift back to 1962. It was the year of her marriage. And it was the year when her husband returned home from a trip to Switzerland to inform her of the move to Dar-al-Kafr. This memory, brought a flood of tears.

1962

"You will be the first sign of our presence in North America." The words of the senior member of the Shura Council had rolled around in the mind of Muhammad Rahimullah since the day two weeks ago when he had attended a meeting at the Islamic Center in Geneva, Switzerland. Finalizing his plans to move to the U.S.A. to pursue post-graduate studies, the gathering brought intellectual heat to the office on what was a cold April morning

Also present were three ranking members of the organization who had flown in from Cairo. The Western hemisphere counterparts were Dr. Abdullah Morgan, M.D., a British epidemiologist tasked with starting the London office, and Anwaar Zakaria, a corporate lawyer and political activist tasked with establishing the Canadian flank of the organization.

The template of the organization was discussed at length and decade incremental goals were established that would begin in 1965.

There was a good reason why the actual goals were not set until three years in advance. The plan would go according to Divine pattern. There would be three years of secrecy just as Prophet Muhammad was involved in the secret call to Islam for three years. He then spent ten additional years in Makkah and the final decade of his life in Madinah.   Twenty-three years. That was the key number. In 1985 the cycle would begin again - three years followed by two decades of goal acquisition. But in this case, 1988 was to be a key year. For it was during the secrecy cycle from 1985-1987 that scholarly players would begin to descend in greater numbers upon the landscape of Canada, the United Kingdom and the United States of America. Regional considerations for the spread of Islam into non-Muslim lands would follow the template. But much latitude was available to address current political tensions and demographic considerations of Muslims already within a migratory status in these nations.

Muhammad Rahimullah, Dr. Morgan and Anwaar Zakaria would begin the work of grounds keeping. Al-Ikhwan would send in the best of their own maturing seed stock from 1985-1987. By 1988, the plant would flourish.

Updated goals would be sent by courier to a small estate in Campione along the eastern shore of Lake Lugano. A predominantly Italian enclave with a few newly arrived Greek residents, the villa had been established as a go-to location for senior members of the organization. Functioning as both a safe house for couriers in transit and boasting an interior design which resembled a primitive construction of later governmental SCIF, the occasional activity would be unlikely to elicit notice. The international neighbors who occupied their own estates in seasonal manner valued and paid a high price for their privacy. With the homes primarily inhabited during the winter season to take advantage of the ski slopes, the warmer months provided a steady flow of estate workers to and from the vacated grounds to maintain their seasonal foliage and stately grandeur. There was no interest by neighbors regarding the smaller estate near the end of the road. The enclave provided a glass bubble type existence for the super nova of society. Blue collar workers interacted carefully with employers. They knew their place in this wealthy society was one which required anonymity and the gift of invisibility. Their employers barely remembered their names. Their children were feared. They were like the sting of a wasp when choosing to flaunt the parental power against the weaker elements of society.

There was a rather hushed story regarding the residence belonging to an Italian family within the enclave. The sixteen year old heir of a telecommunications fortune had raped the fourteen year old daughter of the housekeeper when she had wandered into the west wing of the home while her mother washed the baseboards in the kitchen. Screams never carry far enough, when wings and stairs provide a shield from the activities of the main house. The housekeeper was given a generous "severance package" to take an early retirement. Her daughter received a full scholarship at a remote British boarding school. The deal was drawn up quite discreetly by a corporate lawyer. When all was said and done the small cadre of workers who populated the landscape retained knowledge of the rape down to the smallest detail. The local constable was none the wiser. Such is the occasional interface between poverty and power, greed and vice.

Great care was taken in securing the employment of two individuals to give a semblance of normalcy to the organizational safe house. A middle-aged and alcoholic British butler had been acquired through an employment agency in Hyde Park. It was his understanding that other than maintaining his small cottage at the far end of the acreage and shopping for his own needs the only true requirement for service would be to buzz through the large metal gate the bi-weekly lawn and garden crew. The actual butler's room was adjacent to the back staircase by the kitchen. A dank affair with lack of adequate ventilation, it had a depressing interior with only one small window affording natural light. The grounds keeper's cottage near the stables was remodeled and has an updated look. It is configured to the size and specifications of a London mews. The south end sported a bed, bookcase and an ox blood recliner. The north side, a compact kitchen with a table, small stove, apartment-sized refrigerator, and dish cupboard. Mr. Robbins requested this space allotment and was thrilled that his request is honored. It was intentional that he was shown the lesser of the two living spaces first.   His contract was generous and included a month-long yearly holiday. Robbins was not elderly, but a life of steady drinking and a cigarette addiction which dated back to age fourteen had taken its toll on him. His skin has a bit of a sallow appearance, and is too leathery for his stated age. The hair is noticeably thinning. It took him about three seconds to pick up the pen and sign the contract when it was skated across the desk to land under his nose.

The nondescript housekeeper was secured from a nearby village. She was paid a full-time salary for daily light cleaning of the estate. She was given the code for the gate and foyer entrance but forbidden the keys for the rooms on the second and third landings. She was to arrive promptly at nine and was to leave by three p.m. each day. Elise Montague was a French woman of small stature, a widow without children. Until the day she was approached for employment at the estate her life had unfolded slowly and in tragic manner like the slow slither of a snake's tail. Her life was one of anonymity.

After her husband's death, Elise ran the small flower shop left to her by Monsieur Montague. But as the Dr. Kevorkian of the plant world she ended up killing off her profits in short order and took up a job as a barmaid at a small neighborhood establishment. With an I.Q. not much higher than her own body temperature and looks shot to hell, the situation seemed utterly bleak. Neither her brain nor her sagging real estate held much appeal except for the most desperate of associates. But she knew that the adage that "one old dog likes another old dog" was true. She satisfied her craving for companionship by volunteering to clean up the small bar area after closing. The bartender had a policy to "never turn it down". Without a standard, he held to no real standard regarding his taste in women. Elise might not be the best, but she showed herself the most willing. As for Elise, she considered the bartender a sweaty ill-mannered lout yet for what he lacked in technique he made up for in exuberance. As he bounced her across the top of the bar, she silently cursed the day she had ever met him. But by the next evening she always found herself brushing up against him again, aggressively showing her availability.

During the summer of 1961 a stylishly dressed woman had approached her regarding a job at the mysterious estate. Complimenting her on the grand manner in which she served the beverages and cleaned the tables, poor Elise had the best of hearts within the worst of fools. She actually swallowed the compliment in its entirety and quickly moved to straighten her apron and run a grubby and slightly nicotine-stained finger across her hairline. Her life as discounted underpaid stoop labor came to a skidding halt. She knew a good deal was on the table and seemed incurious regarding the scant details of the oblique offer. She would receive a full wage for a minimum of work. Two days later she found herself shopping for three new uniforms and a good pair of walking shoes. The next day she took her small car down the isolated road to the home of her new employer. She later considered this particular day as one in which Providence shined down on her with grace.

For the first time in her life she was now able to support herself in a manner which seemed a dream. Compared to what had been a prior miserable existence of forty-nine years, Elise now considered herself the most fortunate of God's creatures. She carefully saved her paychecks. She intended to return to her native France in ten years if her luck held out. As is the manner of the undereducated she knew the mechanics of savings and simple math. She knew how to hoard her funds. But the word "stock" made her think of chicken soup. As has been mentioned, Elise was on the shallow end of the gene pool. But she certainly wasn't an idiot. So little by little, her savings became substantial.

Robbins and Montague grasped in a somewhat intuitive manner their compensation was commensurate to their ability to keep their mouths shut. In the case of the butler, he had been specifically chosen for his weakness for intoxicants. His employer made it clear that alcohol was never to be brought into the main house. But in odd manner, every Friday a delivery of an assortment of alcoholic spirits was brought to the gate of the mansion. His full name was always on the package. Carried along in the basket of an area lad with an old postman's bicycle Holmes always gave the boy a small coin for his service. The lad considered himself lucky because the pub owner also paid him for his errand.

The housekeeper had been chosen for the weakness in her gene pool. God had not granted her intellect. This was all the better, for the scheme of things and true nature of the use for the house.

Robbins and Montague chatted amiably regarding the discretion required for their jobs. The estate was a corporate retreat for an unknown entity based out of Egypt. They whispered about patent technology and research and development. These were the words which they were fed when the occasional entourage of businessmen made an appearance at the estate. Both were placed under tight surveillance for the first three months after their retention. Neither of them spoke except in the broadest and vaguest terms regarding their employer. Montague was overheard speaking to the grocery clerk in a rather imperious tone, "Yes, my employers are involved in research and development." The surveillance was shut down and activity at the compound increased. The businessmen arriving on weekends wore Western-style clothing, and spoke a multitude of languages with Arabic and German being the most notable. Robbins and Montague would look at each other knowingly and whisper, "Research and development."

The Secret Call

"You will be the first sign of our presence in North America." The words rolled around in Muhammad's head again as he rounded the corner to see the high white wall surrounding a large home at the end of a secluded lane. Pulling up to the gate he tapped his horn lightly. A moment later the large iron gate swung open and he maneuvered his vehicle toward the port-cochere.

Dr. Abdullah Morgan waved at him from the doorway. "As-Salamu Alaykum, Muhammad. Come in and let us begin a bit of preliminary training." When Muhammad entered the area designated as the classroom something changed in his psyche. It was subtle. He scarcely recognized the signal, but it was there. He recognized the signal in the countenance of his counterparts. They were no longer in Switzerland. They were scarcely aware of the Gregorian calendar. The year became that of the Hijra. They were about to engage a lifelong struggle. Muhammad saw the spark of excitement in the faces of all the men.

By the end of the day, Muhammad was exhausted. The cadre of men had taken a break for prayers.

Other than that, their nourishment had been small dishes containing an odd number of dates and milk which was served from beautiful goat skins. The moderator for the session that day had reminded the men that by emulating the Prophet they would be better equipped to enter the challenging labyrinth of the political process in the West. The moderator spoke in a quiet voice, barely audible.

His style of delivery was intentional. "Just as we are to recite the Qur'an in a measured tone, we must also move in a measured and quiet manner within the West. We do not move as a lion, but we move as a panther."

The scholarly topic of the day was a review of the prophecies of Islam, specifically eschatological considerations. Dr. Yusuf Khan was renowned for his expertise in such matters and had flown straight from a conference in Munich to the meeting in Switzerland. When asked if he felt the need to rest he had responded kindly, "The Sufi is not easily conquered by jet lag. Five hours of sleep a night is sufficient for my frame."

Muhammad Rahimullah clung to every word spoken by Dr. Khan. He had seen with his own eyes the decadence of the West. The women were dressed with bare arms and showing their legs. Some even dared to flaunt their breasts and bellies. Alcohol was readily available. Movie theaters dotted the commercial districts. Signs of innovation were everywhere. Muhammad had allowed his thoughts to wander a bit and suddenly became aware of the voice of the instructor.

"The Prophet Muhammad (PBUH) gave us this prophecy in the Mudkhal by Ibn al-Hajj:

'Prayers will be neglected, carnal desires will be pursued, and transgressors will become leaders. It will not be possible to distinguish the faithful from the false, telling lies will become desirable, payment of Zakah will be taken as a burden, the believer will be deemed the most disgraceful and he will be pained at seeing evils all around. His heart will melt as salt in water but he will not be able to say anything. Rain will do no good; it will fall out of season. Males will commit adultery with males, and females with females. Women will dominate. The offspring will disobey their parents, friend will treat his friend badly, and sins will be taken lightly. Mosques will have external decorations and beauty and there will be worshippers too, but there will be hypocrisy and mutual enmity in their hearts. There will appear a people from the West who will dominate the weak among my people...."

Every word of the prophecy was true. He had seen it all with his own eyes. The homosexuals walked openly on the streets of the West. The women were barely clad. The children were brash and disrespectful in public. The people of the West sought to dominate and dilute the weak of his people. As Muhammad continued to listen to the lecture he felt himself becoming hypervigilant. The feeling was both draining and invigorating.

When Muhammad finally went to bed that night his last thought was to eagerly await the thin white line along the horizon. It would be time to start another training session. It would be the beginning point of a new day of surveying the tasks and challenges which awaited him in North America.

1963

Love comes slowly at times. But lust happens in an instant, like a bolt of lightning from a cobbled sky. In the case of Robbins and Montague, lust knocked on the year anniversary date of their employment. The butler liked the bite of hard liquor. But it had been years since he had enjoyed the slap of a good sexual roust.

Elise had allowed the memories of her former life to slowly fade. She became engrossed in the light cleaning of a home which she came to view as her own. Lovingly dusting the large mirror in the foyer she would then stop to admire herself. She would seat herself on a sofa in the living room and sip tea, imagining she entertained an important neighbor. The imaginary friend usually took the form of one of the matronly women who peered out at her from the pages of a weekly gazette which included a page simply titled, "Society". Her latest companion was a woman who had sported a red suit with a hat to match, red lips and cheeks highlighted with a glittery barfly pink.

22

As of late, Montague had also taken up the odd habit of bringing along her bath salts and bathing in the large claw-foot tub which dominated a downstairs master suite. Somewhere along the way, she began to imagine herself as an estate manager as opposed to a housekeeper. She began to wear perfume, quit biting her nails and paid for a pedicure. Her eyebrows were plucked to look like towering Roman arches and her earlobes sported small pearl earrings. She would straighten her uniform before she answered the doorbell.

Robbins began to pick up the scent of a cornered female in the manner which all beasts examine their prey from afar prior to physical acquisition. He began to part his remaining hair a bit more carefully and took to trimming his moustache. He bought a new tie and discarded his scuffed shoes for a new pair. While the awareness of the other began with Robbins, the very nature of such awareness creates a magnetic pull. Physical attraction is the strangest of emotional beasts. And that beast now took up residence in the corners of the psyche of two lonely souls with plenty of time and a truckload of libido which needed unloading.

Both employees had just received a most generous bonus from their employer. The unexpected nature of the windfall placed them in excellent spirits. The beast in Elise quickly sensed opportunity and she took a long bath, applying perfumed lotion to her body in such generous amounts that there was little doubt as to the "Vacancy" sign on her real estate. Carefully examining her front porch and back porch in the mirror she assessed that her value would go up after a couple of drinks. The beast in Robbins went to the barber for a close shave followed by a trip to a department store to purchase an assortment of chocolates. So it was with firm sense of purpose that Robbins invited Elise to join him in celebration. And it was with a feigned surprise the offer was gleefully accepted.

After a long and boisterous evening of sharing wine and stories, Elise claimed extreme dizziness and the need for some fresh air. Stumbling into the darkness which covered the estate she vaguely remembered removing her clothes. When daylight cracked her first smile Elise awakened first. Robbins was snoring into her ear with an arm slung across her breasts. Her back itched ferociously and her hair felt damp. Slowly standing, she laughed quietly with the thought that she had never seen a naked butler. Without his stuffy little tweed suit and vest, he looked quite the ordinary man. It took her a bit of time to find her undergarments. Locating her slip thrown under a bush she began to remember the performance of a chaotic little dance across the lawn. Suddenly, a shyness and sense of decorum took over. She located all of Robbins clothing and folded them neatly and placed them to the side of his head. As he continued to snore into the grass she realized that her apron was still knotted neatly around his neck. Elise retrieved a vague memory of apron ties wrapped around her hands and what at the time seemed like the ride of Paul Revere. She was overcome with laughter as she remembered yelling, "The British are comin', the British are comin'" and his ridiculous response, "Let 'em come, Elise!" Her last memory of the event was of vomiting into the grass. Such is the nature of drunken sex and the aftermath. Alternating between cursing and giggling she finally made sense of things in the best manner which her brain allowed and said under her breath, "What's done is done." She made the sign of the cross and purposed to buy a new rosary. Carefully unknotting the apron from Robbins neck she gave him a gentle pat on the cheek. She fled toward her vehicle as a bout of queasiness settled into the back of her throat.

Robbins was quite stricken with Elise and remembered quite a bit more of their evening. His liver had long become used to the daily freight of alcohol. He had known that each drink for him would hit Elise with double the punch. So his memories of what had transpired were more to savor than what Elise had remembered. Determined that what had seemed a one course meal should become a standard buffet he showered her with flowers from the gardens and choppy arthritic tunes wheezed out on his old accordion.

Elise had taken to carrying her rosary in the pocket of her dress and would run her fingers across the beads in furious manner whenever she saw Robbins. The bartender was on her socioeconomic level. For a reason she couldn't define the gratuitous nature of their relationship had not gutted her with a sense of guilt. In strange manner, the guilt of her night with Robbins didn't hit her when she put on her apron every morning. It hit when she took it off. Her brain being what is was, she never quite figured out the connection. But she was acutely aware that with Robbins she felt a level of danger and a vulnerable weakness which she had never felt with any other man. He played an accordion. He had a beautiful tenor voice and once he quoted a poem by John

Donne as he handed her a bouquet of flowers. She was not worthy of him and because she was not worthy, it made her feel like a thief to take up with such a genteel and educated man.

Robbins was not one to be deterred. Elise finally cast aside her defensive self-righteousness which she had assumed since the evening of frolic. It so happened that one afternoon as she was burning a candle to the Virgin Mary in the small chapel of the local parish that the wind coming in from an open window blew the flame out. Twice. Superstitious by nature she whispered to nobody in particular, "If the flame goes out a third time it will be a sign that I am to give my love to Robbins. He needs me." When the flame was extinguished the third time she arose from her knees. Placing a bit extra into the crude wooden box which had a small plaque above it reading "Alms for the Poor", she then headed to an area beauty shop to treat herself to a bit of hair color. If she was to be with Robbins she wanted to look like a woman befitting a man of his position. With the wisps of gray washed out of her hair she continued along to the lingerie shop to pick out a new gown. White was for angels and she was determined to play the devil. Black was too bold and red too passionate a flair for her age. She settled on the average cotton gown with small lavender flowers. Pleased with her purchase and her newly found freedom from conscience she stopped at the liquor shop to buy a bottle of whiskey for Robbins. Catching a glimpse of herself in the store mirror she smiled mischievously at her image. Then, she stuck out her tongue.

The human genome is the most mysterious of treasure maps. A man gifted with physical strength may find his weakness to be an eroding self doubt. He looks good on the court or the field but might prove a disaster in the corporate board room. He can make the instant decisions involving sweat but not the robust decisions with long term consequences. The woman with great beauty may have a personality which flows along the shallows. She becomes an arm ornament for her husband to later be treated as a cheap objet d'art no longer worthy of his adoration. He takes up with the intellectual mistress and the beauty is of a more fascinating nature. It is not her physical frame which is the biggest draw but the combined strength and vulnerability of the emotional frame intertwined with high intelligence. But the most arresting and trouble-prone of gene maps is a lack of genius married to insatiable curiosity. Such was the case with Elise. She had been a ferocious snoop from a very young age. It had bothered her from the beginning that she was denied access to the rooms on the second and third landing of the estate. To be sure, the spaciousness of the first floor, the grandeur of the art work and appointment of the living areas on the lower level was a feast for the eyes. The kitchen was spacious and the china cabinet filled with enough place settings to host a sizable party. But each time she climbed the stairs to the second and third landings it irked her immensely. She rattled the doorknobs and would find them firmly locked. Throwing her hands up, she vented her disgust with a blue streak of French curses.

Finding a spare room key became an obsession for Elise. One day a key was found taped neatly to the back of the frame of a picture in the abandoned butler's quarters on the first floor. Elise had wandered into the room and reached to sweep a cobweb away when the nail of the frame gave way and the picture crashed to the floor. Elise had proudly crowed to Robbins, "It was the last place I looked!" She seemed unaware that when an object is located the hunt will cease.

Wishing for new levels of adventure the lovers tried the key in all of the doors. It opened the middle bedroom on the third floor for greater sexual adventures. The room was quite lovely with a large balcony which had a rather grotesque stone gargoyle crouched in the corner and a lush trail of honeysuckle which climbed the trellis along the wall to cascade over the gargoyle's brow. The vibrant orange flowers had the look of a gypsy skirt and the diamond lit sky at night was beautiful to behold. The couple would take their wine bottle and glasses upstairs. After a roustabout in the bed they would head to the balcony for a smoke and a drink. One night the flare of passion which started in the room moved to the balustrade beyond the French doors. When Elise lost her grip she was somersaulted to the pavement below. By the time Robbins got to her she was dead. Her broken neck gave her body the look of a broken doll. A small trickle of blood seeped from one of her ears and pooled around her pearl earring. Robbins had the presence of mind to dress her, drag her back into the house and carefully lay her at the base of the staircase. He even tried to position her like he had found her on the cement. He also placed on of her shoes at the top of the staircase, and the other a third of the way down the landing. In a panic he ran to the far end of the property to drop the room key into an abandoned well.   He then waited 2 hours to call the police.

The village medical examiner was a burly and unfriendly man. He was even more irritated after being called out by the local constable. He had just ordered his second pint of ale from the village pub. Not one to be bothered because of one unknown dead housekeeper he finished his ale and ordered a third before he finally lifted his corpulent frame from the wooden stool. He took his time at the urinal and then also stopped at the gate of the home to aim a stream of urine at the brass plate which identified the address. Blue-collar to the marrow, he resented the wealthy for reasons he could not quite explain. The chip on his shoulder had been there for as long as he could remember.

His father had been a railroad porter. He carried the baggage of the wealthy to the trains which took them to the ski resorts rising up from the snow clad landscape like gigantic piles of logs. With only a fourth grade education, the father had the working-class pride which belongs to those with cracked knuckles and scuffed boots. But it was at times accompanied by excessive bravado and a distinctly suspicious nature toward wealth in general. He lived in a working class neighborhood which solidified his belief system. The men were all like crabs floating in a plastic bucket of water at the beach. If one crab finally managed to crawl his way to the top of the bucket, before he could escape to the larger world, another crab would quickly reach with its claw to pull him back into the water. So it was that if any wife was spotted with a new dress, or a child with a new pair of shoes, the neighborhood men would boisterously gather around their comrade the following payday and demand a round of drinks from their friend. Glasses would be held high and toasts made. Another round of drinks followed and all would eventually stumble home singing the praises of their buddy. On a purely primitive and subliminal level they understood they had pulled the crab back into the bucket. Although the medical examiner had surpassed his father's wildest dreams, he also retained the unique scaffolding of thought possessed by the chronically undereducated poor. The medical examiner thought himself to be a man of the world. He was really just a reflection of dear old dad.

He had acquired a comfortable home with the guarantee of a nice pension awaiting him at age sixty. The family took a holiday each year. His children would all attend college. But estates which were larger than his childhood elementary school irked him. Any sense of intimidation brought the darkness of his psyche to the forefront and the bias instilled by his nominally literate father took hold.

The wind was blowing wildly as he stood outside the estate pissing furiously upon the brass plate and so it was that he made his appearance with alcohol on his breath and his shirt a bit damp. Taking in the scene quickly he surmised that a death spiral beginning at the top of the staircase was the cause of fatal injury. Taking one look at Elise he simply stated, "Poor damn thing. It looks as if she has broken her neck. Bag her up and take her to the morgue." The official cause of death read, "C3 fracture sustained from fall down a staircase." The village coroner never even unbuttoned Elise's blouse. She had no kin and nobody would miss the wretch. But he did stick his sweaty hand down into the bra to see if the housekeeper had hidden any money under her breasts. He had seen his mother do it on many occasions. After also rummaging through her skirt pockets, poor Elise was given into the care of the local parish priest and placed in a pauper's grave at the back of the cemetery.

The young policeman who had been at the scene with the constable and the coroner was an idealistic young fellow. He felt it his duty to send a small note to internal affairs. The accusation was dereliction of duty because of the constable's lack of interest in collecting evidence or even properly interrogating the witness. When internal affairs received the memo he received a hearty reprimand and returned to his post a bit wiser regarding his organization.

Robbins placed a small obituary in the daily newspaper and notified his employer of the tragedy at hand. Elise had recently changed her will and left all of her earthly belongings to Robbins. When the solicitor handed him a check for what was in his lover's bank account he went to the nearest bar and drank for hours. "God," he thought, "How I miss my little French flower." Six weeks later he returned to England.

Twilight

Robbins was placed under surveillance on his return to England. Late one night in a small pub near his home he was overheard singing in a drunken voice to no one in particular. "My little French flower fell over the rail, fell over the rail, over the rail." This was duly reported and an area thug was located who agreed to slip a sedative into Robbins final drink of the evening in return for what he was assured was "a shoebox full of cash" under the bed of his victim.

The following night as Robbins was stumbling home he found himself accompanied by another man, this one seemingly quite drunk himself. The next morning Robbins was found floating in the Thames. Accidental drowning secondary to inebriation, was the official report. The shoebox of cash planted under the bed disappeared. A "grieving cousin" then made quick work of removing any evidence of Robbins' life during the time of his employment in Switzerland. Problem solved.

Dr. Abdullah Morgan was attending the final day of meetings for an infectious diseases conference in Geneva.

When he received the news of Robbins' death, he grimaced slightly. It had been a stressful week. It was complicated by a calendar of activities which included seeking suitable replacements for the two prior employees of the estate. A day before the beginning of the conference he had worked his way through multiple employment files for prospective staff for the safe house. After the near disaster with the prior two staff members, he was in no mood to pair any middle-aged couple with libido issues. The unfortunate situation with Robbins and Montague had been figured out with no need for detective work on the part of Dr. Morgan. Robbins had left a bottle of wine on the balcony and an empty bottle sat next to it. Eye glasses with a feminine frame were nestled into the honeysuckle. He would not have noticed it, had the glint of the sun not caught the glass at the right moment. Disgusted, Dr. Morgan disposed of the bottles and noted the rumpled state of the bed.

He finally settled on two individuals for a second interview: a twice-divorced mother in her early fifties with a deaf son in his late twenties. The woman and her son would both live on site with Mrs. Baehler residing in the servant's quarters on the first landing and her son moving into Robbins' space. She would perform light housekeeping and her son, Eric Baehler, would function as the full-time gardener. All other seasonal staff had been dispatched with a modest final bonus. Mrs. Baehler and her son were people of solitude. Neither of them had a friend in the world except each other. Eric had quite a knack for lip-reading. And during the interview it was rare that Mrs. Baehler needed to sign back and forth with him to keep the interview flowing properly. He spoke in the monotone manner of the hearing impaired and Dr. Morgan wondered lazily if the future would hold a cure for his disease. It was just a passing thought. The good doctor had only one real interest and it was the study of bacteria. When he wasn't in the research lab he was still engaged in studying bacteria. But it was the study of political bacteria – more specifically, the super bug otherwise known as the Western allies, which intrigued him.

Dr. Morgan was pleased with his final determination and only one task remained. He would spend a day at the estate to follow an area locksmith around as he changed all of the locks on the upper landing. The private spaces would be checked to assure that nothing had been disturbed or taken. Damn the butler and the lascivious housekeeper. They had caused sufficient reason for alarm.

In two days he would take flight to Saudi Arabia. It was the season of the Hajj. It always gave him great pleasure to throw rocks at the devil. He would reserve a rock for the sin of zina with Montague's name attached. Robbins could not be blamed. He had been seduced by a woman. Men must be careful regarding women. They could not be trusted when alone with a man. A woman could seduce with a look, perfume or the sound of their laughter. Distracted by his thoughts, Dr. Morgan determined to call his wife prior to leaving for the Hajj.

The Hajj

Dr. Muhammad Rahimullah, Dr. Abdullah Morgan, and Anwaar Zakaria embraced as they met at the entrance of the Prophet's mosque in Al-Madina Al-Munawwara. It was the 7th of Zul-Hijjah and on the following day they would be in Makkah to begin the five days of rituals in and around Makkah which comprise part of the pilgrimage.

All three men had made the pilgrimage in prior years. But there was a sense of freshness when considering the significance of the landmarks. Whether it was Jabal Al-Rahman on the plain of Arafat, the spring known as ZamZam, or the area with the three obelisks which symbolize the three times in which Satan came to Ibrahim and his son Isma'il, the men looked forward to every moment shared together – in adoration of Allah. The previous few years had cemented the bond of brotherhood. Like the Qu'ran, they were a firmly cemented structure known as the Ummah.

None of the men believed the Prophet had been unlettered. They considered him highly educated for his time and place in history – a statesman, strategist and military general, all wrapped up in the cloak of a prophet. Neither did they have any sense of angst regarding those who considered abrogation of the Qur'anic text a mere exercise in situational ethics. They believed the complete Qur'an was downloaded into the leader of their faith at an instant in time. He merely released the word of god when the time was sensitive, his audience malleable to the message. The original text of the Qur'an was in heaven and the Qur'an on earth represented the active voice of their god and creator.

The three men were deeply immersed in the study of the Qur'anic Sciences: Sunnah, Seerah, Dalail, Maghazi, Shamail, etc.

Dr. Muhammad Rahimullah, in particular, had physically handled many of the ancient manuscripts of Islam. On his shelf was a complete volume by Pakistani poet, Hafiz Jalandhari, who composed the national anthem of Pakistan. The monumental work of Jalandhari is the entire biography of the Prophet in the form of Na'at.

But Dr. Rahimullah, Ph.D was fascinated with the Shamail, which describes the attributes of his leader.

The books of Shamail recorded the number of grey hairs in the beard of the Prophet, fourteen in number. Each time Muhammad Rahimullah stroked his beard and then grasped it with his fist, he would remember the number. During Eid-ul-Fitr the prior year his wife had presented him with slippers with two double stripes. He was thrilled. He was familiar with "Shamail al-Tirmizi" and took great delight in emulating all aspects of the prophet's personality, dress, dinner habits such as eating an odd number of date fruit, and giving the required response when someone sneezed. He was perfectly mannered and groomed in proper manner at all times.

Dr. Abdullah Morgan, M.D. is a revert to Islam. So he was not so greatly inclined to the manners of the Prophet. His interest was in the battles of the Muslims. Just as he battled the bacteria in the lab, he imagined the world laden with the bacteria in Dar-ul-Kafr. Political bacteria must be eradicated. Either that, or subjugated to the point it is now longer able to cause harm to the host called Ummah – vicegerent of the world.

Dr. Abdullah Morgan, M.D. had been named Trevor Morgan III at birth. His grandfather had been a pediatrician. His own father was a plastic surgeon who still ran a lucrative practice from an office near

Kensington Palace. Dr. Morgan had been raised in a family with only social religious leanings. Attendance of any religious event, whether it was for Christmas mass or the baptism of a baby, was as perfunctory as scheduling a dental appointment.

During a family holiday in Germany, Trevor Morgan was introduced to the daughter of one of his father's professional associates, a young lady named Dhalia Saeed. She was enchanting, mystical and had a musical laugh which bounced off the walls. He was only seventeen the first time he laid eyes on Dhalia, but she reminded him of his maternal grandmother, whom he dearly loved. They became steady friends. After Trevor's second year of medical school he proposed to Dhalia and she readily accepted. His immediate family moved gracefully through the crisis which presented when the family crest of the Morgan family became one which now boasted a man with the name of Abdullah, the name he had chosen after his shahada. But it was his grandfather, who never spoke to him again. He was the third Trevor Morgan; the third doctor in the family. The family patriarch would have none of it. As for Abdullah Morgan, he was now the servant of Allah. He began to immerse himself in his new community. It was as if his life as Trevor Morgan had never existed. Nothing existed that had not been corrupted. After his declaration that he was a Muslim he was a changed man.

His personality was not like that of Dr. Rahimullah who was a person of grace. His posture was one of forcefulness. Islam must come by force. And force came from the vehicle of saraya. He was intent on forming raiding parties which would infiltrate the political structure of the British Parliament. The beachhead into the United Kingdom had been established in 1962, in the same manner that the seed had first been scattered into north America the same year. He longed for political transitions in Great Britain which would bring Muslims into their rightful place. There could be no assimilation to the West; only expansion of Islam as Deen, an all encompassing way of life. Islam was a gestalt. It was the gestalt he understood through the eyes of a deeply thoughtful and highly intelligent scientist. His work as an epidemiologist in one of the top labs in London allowed him ample time for political activities in the evening and on weekends.

Anwaar Zakaria was a former member of Hizb-ut-Tahrir. Seeing a lack of political potency in the leadership, he set his flag to the rebel's mast and joined the more vibrant political organization. His distinct area of interest was the miracles of his leader. He knew it would take a miracle for the Caliphate to ever be established again. But he wished to be part of the vicegerency of Allah which brought about the necessary changes for Islamic dominance. His current organization had the feel of the Great Wall of China. An alliance existed which networked across the globe. The ranks ran deep and the ranks were close. There was no need to worry if one foot soldier fell out of place on the wall. The one behind him would step forward to take his place, the one in the third place would move to the second, so on and so forth. There were front office leaders and back office unrecognized leadership. The public face protected the private leadership. The organization was completely impenetrable. It was the secretiveness and impenetrability of the organization which appealed to his psyche. He had endured a complicated vetting process for acceptance. He now found himself increasingly tasked with collateral activities. He felt himself strong on the stalk. Islam permeated his psyche.

So it was that the three men hugged each other a second and a third time before they stepped inside the Prophet's mosque. They were part of something bigger than themselves. They were part of a historical legend. No longer did they live in the United States, Canada or the United Kingdom. When they stepped across the threshold of the mosque, they were time travelers. They landed right back in the seventh century. Eternity was in their hearts. Transitioning through the centuries required little effort. It only required faith.

All three men had already entered a state of Ihram at one of the defined points called Meeqat, or along the points which were connecting points for those coming to observe Hajj. For people coming from the north the Meeqat is Dhul-Hulaifa, which is near Madinah. From the northwest the point is Juhfa near the city of Yanbu'. Those traveling from the northeast pass through Dhat Al-Iraq or Mahdat Iraq. For people coming from the east it is Qarn Al-Manazil and those arriving from the south pass through Yalamlam, which is near Taif.

The colleagues were now each clad in two pieces of unstitched cloth; one cloth around the shoulders and covering the upper body to the waist, and the second cloth from the waist to below the knees.

There are prohibited activities once in a state of Ihram. On minor scale, no shaving, cutting the nails, plucking hair, or use of perfumeries by men or women.

The prohibition extends to include sexual abstinence and no hunting activities.

The men had recited the Talbiyah as they entered Makkah from their various entry points: Here I am, Oh Allah, here I am. You have no partner. I am here. Indeed all praise and all grace belong to You and all sovereignty. There is no partner, here I am.....

On the 8th of Dhul-Hijjah the men entered Makkah and headed into the surging throng of humanity heading to Ka'bah to perform the Tawaf of arrival. Beginning at the Black Stone in the corner of the building the three men began to walk around the Ka'bah in counterclockwise manner. They did this seven times. An hour later they completed the circumambulation and then proceeded to perform the two ra'kah of salat.

Leaving the Ka'bah they hurried to complete the next step of their journey. They walked between the hills which were walked by their ancestor, Hagar. The walk between the hills is done seven times, and is called Sa'ie. It begins at the hill of Safa and the walk is toward the hill of Marwah. It was within this space that Hagar ran back and forth seeking water for her son. She had seated him on the ground and on her return from a frantic search the spring was bubbling up between the legs of her small son. Shouting "Collect, collect!" she cupped her hands into the growing pool of water.

The men then proceeded to the Mina valley on foot. A tent awaited them and in it they would spend the night, but without much sleep. Sleep was light, if at all, for the three friends. After the sun was up on the 9th Dhul Hijjah the men began their travel to the plain of Arafat. In the early afternoon they performed Salat Al-Zuhr and 'Asr., two ra'kah each. Then they settled in to listen to the imam deliver the khutbah. After sunset the men arose and traveled to Muzdalifah, a valley near to the one in which they had spent the night. Once there, they performed their Maghrib and Isha Salat. That night, they slept very well. Each of them carried a small pouch. In it, they had placed forty-nine pea-sized pebbles for stoning the three Satan obelisks in Mina.

The 10th of Dhul Hijjah was a beautiful day and the day of Eid Al-Adha for the rest of the world. There is no Eid for the pilgrims. It is a day of sacrifice. After the completion of the animal sacrifice the three men cut their hair, took a shower and changed out of their two white garments. What would remain would be the farewell Tawaf around the Ka'bah. From there, the three men would catch their flight home.

The Spreading Canopy

Anwaar Zakaria stepped off his flight and hailed a taxi at the curb. His baggage was heavy. He was laden with gifts for the brothers at the mosque. There were small gifts for the men he prayed with every day. He had sets of postcards for this group. These were men in his mosque who were new immigrants. They had saved for years to come to Canada. The mosque had a small fund, Al-Ansar, which assisted with initial expenses for these families. But beyond that, the families struggled along. It would be years before some of the male head of household could scrape together the funds for Hajj. Nicer gifts had been carefully selected for   members of the Shura Council. He was a part of them. They were a part of him. They were a firmly cemented structure, just like the Qur'an. Nothing could move them nor deter their sense of purpose. There was a staccato cadence of exhilaration in his psyche. It showed in his quickened pace as he moved through the Toronto Pearson International Airport. His wallet was empty but he felt as if his feet no longer touched the earth. He remembered the words of the Qur'an concerning the benefits of Hajj.

Memories whirled through his mind and he was unsure which was his favorite.   Eyes searching the teeming mass at the Ka'bah and performing the Tawuf of arrival had swept him straight back into the seventh century.   But throwing rocks at the devil had stitched him into the eternal timeline of his Islamic history. The meals, scents, the sights and sounds, drinking ZamZam water, had provided his soul with nourishment. To read about Hajj was one thing. The sensory experience of the event was something entirely different. The prior time he attended Hajj it had been with his father at his side. In fearful adoration he followed the instructions given by his father. Bi'dah. It was a most beautiful thing. To be the slave of Allah, Lord of the Worlds, the god with ninety-nine beautiful names with one unknown, gave him a sense of purpose. He began to recite Al-Kursi as the cab sped him toward home.

When he arrived, his widowed mother was in the kitchen making some of her signature lamb kebabs. The fame of her deft cooking skill was well-known in the community. It was also the downfall of her bachelor son. He had not yet fulfilled half of his religion because, quite frankly, he had not visited the home of any eligible young lady and tasted a meal comparable to the ones created by his own mother. But he was also an only surviving child. A good child must care for the welfare of his parents. Zakaria had lost his father and younger brother in the manner in which fate can deliver bad news in a double punch style. The family was returning from a wedding late one evening. A light rain was falling. A vehicle speeding through a red light had T-boned the family vehicle on the driver's side. Their vehicle had managed to hydroplane sideways right into a telephone pole. His father had been properly belted into place. But he suffered a head injury with a C2 fracture. He died on the scene. His brother Ismail was seated in the back seat behind his father. He suffered massive internal bleeding and died a day later in the pediatric intensive care unit of an area hospital. Anwaar's mother had suffered a broken collarbone. Anwaar had only a few bruises on his upper arms and a contusion on his right hip to show for the accident. He felt guilty because he imagined his brother had cushioned him from death.

What Anwaar Zakaria really remembered of the post accident events was the incessant barking of a large dog, an animal which had the look of a looming dark shadow a few feet from the accident site. It barked and barked and barked. There seemed to be no master nearby. The animal did not appear to have either a collar or a tag. For a month after the death of his brother, Anwaar would enter the powerful substratum known as REM sleep where he would see a large and shaggy black dog inches from his face. The dog would move closer and its saliva would drip on his shirt. He would feel it suck the breath out of his lungs and take it as his own. And then he would awaken, drenched in sweat and with the smell of fear on his skin. He would stumble into the shower and turn on the cold tap and feel it stream over his hair and across his back. When he began to shiver, he would step out to towel off and crawl back into his bed. The terror of his dream was the trauma from his wound. It was a wound which had never quite healed. And it had made him afraid to love again. Love was a cruel master which sent black dogs to haunt his sleep. Love was an emotion which brought unnecessary vulnerability. The keloid scar across his psyche now made him both love his mother, and at times, distance himself from her. The years had been emotionally lean for him since the death of his father.

After the accident, Anwaar and his mother visited an Islamic lawyer to properly settle the estate. Anwaar took his portion and quietly scouted the neighborhoods of

Toronto for an upgraded home. He needed something more befitting his mother and what had been his father's status in the community. But it must also wear the cloak of humility, just as had been the manner of his father. The home he chose had a subdued elegance. The guest bedroom would be used as a library and home office. His mother would use the downstairs master suite. Anwaar would have the solitude required to roam about the second landing. Shortly after his mother completed her period of mourning, the moving trucks began to arrive. That had been five years ago. It had been a good decision. The mosque was a short distance away. Within walking distance, a modest halal grocer dispensed the best cuts of meat and a fresh supply of fruit and vegetables. Most importantly, his mother had befriended two other widows in the neighborhood. Their status as widows was a respected one, their children were grown, and they had plenty of time to sit around solving the world's problems over cups of tea and plates of sweets.

Anwaar let himself into the home quietly on his return. The smell of meat cooked with a liberal quantity of spices filled the air. He felt the saliva flood his mouth as his nostrils savoured the scent. Kissing his mother on the cheek as he entered the kitchen, Anwaar produced two packages with a flourish. "A gift of dates from Saudi Arabia. They are the sweetest in the world. And also, here are some of the finest pistachios from Iran which I purchased from a side street vendor." His mother patted his cheek with fondness and her eyes brimmed with love. As soon as he left the room she picked up the phone to call one of her friends. Anwaar smiled as he listened to the conversation as it floated up the stairs. Beyond being quite the gossip, his mother was a complete braggart concerning her only remaining son. She had not opened the package of dates yet, but he heard the joyful sound of her voice ring out, "Why, they are the best dates I have ever set my teeth into and you must come and share them with me later today!" Anwaar laughed uproariously as he threw open the windows of his office to take the staleness out of the room.

Heading to his computer, Anwaar checked his email file. Ahhh, there it was. Decoding the string of Hadith, he gave a little smile. The pouch had transitioned safely to Hyderabad. It had been on quite a journey, and it remained in good company. The Guardian was doing well.

When the moon was fleeing along her path to make way for the rising sun Anwaar was still seated in his office. A cup of cold tea was beside him. He was beginning to feel the exhaustion of his trip. As he performed his ablution for the Fajr prayer his thoughts returned to his circumambulation of the Ka'bah. The thousands of bodies pressed against each other had a distinct smell. Even the air within the valley of Mina retained the same crisp odor of the clean garments worn by the men.

Prophet Muhammad had moved out from Hira, a four by 1.75 meter space down the slopes of An-Nour to establish the law of Allah. He survived the confines of an economic blockade.   His wife Khadijah relied on the smuggled wheat from Hakeem bin Hizam. The Prophet sent immigrants to Abyssinia to escape the persecution against Muslims. He later fled Makkah with Abu Bakr and made Madinah the seat of government. He proclaimed the vastness of Allah's earth. But his life had been one of prophetic confinement. The Muslims were now 1.5 billion strong. The thought gave him comfort. It was for this reason that Anwaar and his mother were living in a vast country known as Canada. But it was time for the Muslims to break free of the confinements of the West.

Anwaar remained alert as he performed his prayers. Exhaustion combined with exhilaration released a cascade of hormonal responses which carried him all the way through breakfast. Kissing his mother on the cheek he said, "I have yet to retire to bed. Perhaps it is needful that I seek a bit of rest before meeting with the brothers." His mother smiled at him with amazement. She was at the time of life that anything less than ten hours of rest left her feeling weakened. Patting her son's cheek she encouraged him to hurry along to bed. "Your clean sheets have not proven useful yet."

Anwaar's mind traveled slowly across a hazy dreamscape. He was in Egypt. The shadows were lengthening across a courtyard. In his hand he held a small object. And then he saw the black dog. Pulling the covers over his head, Anwaar groaned. With a tremendous act of his will he returned to examining what was in his hand.

1985

"The Muslim does not think in term of years. Our thoughts are embedded in eternity. The timeline is more fluid and with less bumps. There is no living on-the-dash, so to speak, as the manner taken in the West. Our counterpart lives on the dash on their tombstones; that curious little hyphen which separates date of birth from date of death and shows man in a finite state. We will win in the end, because we are on the side of the Lord of the Worlds. Our Rasool recited the Qur'an. He gave us Allah's words. We are better qualified to lead. Our leadership sees the unseen, the eternal aspects of Allah."

Muhammad Qutb touched his beard lightly with the index and middle finger of his right hand. He then picked up his tea and sipped the remaining few drops. Turning the cup sideways toward his audience he continued speaking.

"The Muslim does not read the tea leaves as is done by the kufr in the West. We read what was written on the leaves of the manuscript, kept by Fatima, daughter of Prophet Muhammad (PBUH).

Our brotherhood did not start with Hassan al-Banna. It did not gain strength with the works of my uterine relation, Sayyid Qutb. The strength was there from the beginning. It began with Prophet Muhammad (PBUH). The Sahabah became the guardians of the Sunnah of the Prophet. We continue as   the reflection of what was, what is and what is to come. Our guide is Prophet Muhammad (PBUH) and our order is based on Divine commands clearly stated in the Qur'an."

The small circle of men shifted their crossed legs a bit to enable the circulation.   They knew that when Muhammad Qutb began to speak he would only retire his speech for one of two reasons. Either is was time for the evening prayers or there was the need to relieve his bladder.

Qutb continued, "We know the Khilafa was patterned after the example of the final Prophet. But prophecy tells of a time for mulkan jabriyyatan – the tyrannical kingship. And who is more tyrannical than the government of the United States of America?" Taking the index and middle finger of his right hand he pulled a piece of lamb and a bit of rice from the edge of the plate. Encouraging his companions to do the same they served themselves in like manner. "Kafa-bi'l – Saifa. Sufficient is the sword for remedy. The sword is unsheathed again. But it is the sword of the pen, the sword of the word. It is sharp when wielded by powerful men. The one hundred and fourteen Surah, the 6,300 ayat are the guide. While the West focuses on the 1/3 of the ayat given after hijra I will teach you to focus on the 2/3 ayat which were given in Makkah. These concepts will hasten our movement into the West." Muhammad Qutb continued to speak and his words captivated his audience. The men were enthralled and each one present considered himself a student of a great man.

Seated within the circle was a new member to this small group of men in Jeddah. Dr. Dawud Malik was a strikingly handsome pharmacist who had received his degree from the Massachusetts College of Pharmacy and Health Sciences. A prestigious institution, the alumni prided themselves on having graduated from the second oldest and the largest pharmaceutical college in the nation. But Dawud considered his time spent obtaining an undergraduate degree in chemistry with a minor in microbiology the best season of his life. During his junior and senior years at Quaid-i-Azam University in Islamabad he headed the student wing of Ja'maat e Islami. The planning meetings were segregated. But during a short conversation with the campus leader for the Muslims sisters he began to feel the strong urges of manhood.   After graduation, he married the woman whose passion matched his own. Maryam was from an honored family. Her father was a minor state bureaucrat with decent ties into the central government. Maryam, for her part, was deeply in love with a man whom she really barely knew. But the reputation of Dawud within Ja'maat gave him star power on campus. On the wedding night she willingly allowed her new husband to assume the ownership of his bed.   It was in the first year of his graduate studies in the U.S. that Dawud Malik laid his eyes on what Allah had hidden in the womb. Maryam gave birth to a son. It seemed appropriate to name the child after his only brother who had died of whooping cough at a young age. Thus it was that Ibrahim made his entrance to the world. Dawud was overcome with fatherly pride. Taking his son in his arms when handed to him for the first time he spoke the Azan to the right ear of his child and the Iqamah to the left ear. Satisfied that he had done his spiritual duty to protect his child from the jinn, the neonate was passed to his mother. Dawud watched as Maryam struggled a bit to get the baby to attach to the nipple. His brothers at the mosque had warned him that women were temperamental during pregnancy, birth and immediately afterward. He suddenly saw his wife glare at him a bit, and then she returned to pushing the baby up against her breast. Dawud thought that the whole thing had the look of suffocation.

The following year, Basil also made his appearance. In 1982, with two sons and a wife in tow Dr. Malik had taken his family on their first trip together for Hajj. It had been ten years since he had entered the United States and he longed to move back to Muslim soil. It was shortly after throwing rocks at the devil that a man who had seemed to be watching him approached quietly with the offer of a business deal. Two months later Dr. Malik had ended his pharmaceutical career at a major hospital in Deerborn, Michigan and found himself seated behind a small desk in the cramped office of a fledgling pharmaceutical supply business. Maryam was not in the happiest of moods as she had learned that she was pregnant with her third child shortly after their arrival in Jeddah. This pregnancy was tough on her too. Almost from the beginning she suffered from hyperemesis. The extreme heat took its toll and twice she was taken to the hospital for intravenous rehydration.

After having given birth to both sons within the sterile confines of a labor room with a blank looking wall she now found herself squatting over a wooden birthing stool with a neighbor lady supporting her back and a midwife yelling in her face to "push harder". Up until this point Maryam had little forgiveness for what her husband had put her through with the move. But when Aisha made her appearance all was forgiven. Maryam secretly believed that there had never been a more beautiful little girl. Naturally, she would never vocalize her words.

It was soon after the arrival in Jeddah that Dr. Malik fell under the spell of Muhammad Qutb. As an avid reader of the works of Al-Mawdudi and also Sayyid Qutb, his loyalty toward a personality moved from a simmer to a boil again. He had fulfilled half of his religious obligation already. His marriage had been a source of strength for his life. Now he considered it his duty to fulfill any remaining obligations. On this day and less than 24 hours after the birth of his daughter, he found himself seated in the presence of a man whom he had grown to greatly respect.

Pausing for a moment to refill his tea, Muhammad Qutb glanced at Dr. Dawud Malik in almost a casual manner, had it not been for such a piercing gaze. He noted a man who seemed strong on the stalk, ready for recruitment. Making his decision, he began to focus quite a few of his comments toward Dr. Malik to assess his response. The way he looked at it, he had time to give the man a bit more backbone. When the time was right, he would send him to Egypt for additional training.

Khalid ibn Abdulaziz al-Misri

Khalid ibn Abdulaziz al-Misri was a fortunate man. As a steel magnate based out of Alexandria he lived in a world of incomparable wealth and luxury. As a member of the largest consortium of steel producers with offices in Cairo, London and New York his travel itinerary allowed for the many side benefits which are available to the unaccompanied business executive.

His first wife was acquired in the years before he attained his stature and prominence. She was the daughter of a noted scholar of Al-Azhar and held narrowly defined views of femininity and sexual expression. She had dutifully produced six children in repetitious nature and the disappointment of four daughters was allayed when her final pregnancy produced identical sons.

Hagar was smart enough. But the final pregnancy had been hard on her and she had not allowed her husband to touch her during that time. Her blame was small, in the lifestyle change of her husband which followed her pregnancy.

63

The power which seduces and tests the souls of men in the boardroom will invariably progress to the power afforded in the bedroom. Money is easy to manipulate. But the manipulation of souls is always the more satisfactory pleasure. Successful men never lack companionship, if that is the bent. And Khalid al-Misri began to take note of the lifestyles of his professional colleagues. "Keep your official wife. Keep her happy and in the dark. And then do whatever you damn well please", was the advice of a European counterpart. Al-Misri had toyed with the idea of infidelity on occasion. But his wife's final pregnancy provided the catalyst to developing a full-blown plan of action. Khalid al-Misri was a man of patience until the moment he chose to act. But when he determined to act, there was no yielding of his will to any other man.

Khalid ibn Abdulaziz al-Misri had been a guest of General al-Walid, head of the Egyptian security forces on several occasions during his wife's final pregnancy. By this time he had amassed the substantial wealth which welcomed him into the top social circles of Cairo and beyond. The General was a discreet business partner involved in asset management of al-Misri's competitors. His monthly retainer by al-Misri was always accompanied by an additional gift of gratitude for the president. It was a "privilege" to do business in Egypt. Al-Misri also understood in terrifying manner what could be the result of falling out of privilege. On the day he had struck the deal with his counterpart he had been invited to the security building in Alexandria. "Khalid!" General al-Walid's voice boomed across his desk as he stood to greet his latest partner in crime. "Let me show you where we deal with the enemies of the state. It is where we do our best work!"   General al-Walid then took al-Misri to the basement caverns where the results of his "best work" were housed. The smell along the corridors of the underground hell was only surpassed by a smell of rotting human flesh when the general requested that a heavy wooden door in the solitary confinement pod be opened so that al-Misri could catch a glimpse of the man inside. In a tone which sounded both sympathetic and disdainful General al-Walid remarked, "Torture and lack of sunshine can do terrible things to a man." With that, he clapped Khalid on the back and said, "You must join me for lunch. I have reserved a room at one of the best restaurants in Alexandria!"

The meal was of such epic proportions – both in bounty and quality – that Khalid began to dread the day he had ever hatched his plan. He remembered the last time he had bribed a prestigious member of the legislature. The man had bitten him hard.

By the time the appointment was over he had agreed to double the price, and what looked like an additional bonus for the general, any time he hauled in one of Khalid's competitors for a short stay at the "Alexandria Hotel".

Eventually though, al-Misri began to appreciate both the necessity and the genius of his plan. It only took a phone call on his end to set the plan in motion. General al-Walid always came through. As al-Misri observed the mechanics of military political power, and indeed, the military men in power who also belonged to his own organization, he had a renewed respect for Egypt's place in the world. Egypt would rise again. Egypt would enslave the Jews again. It was mere convenience that the Jews had stupidly placed themselves on Egypt's doorstep. There would be no mythological parting of the Red Sea for a future salvation.

During one visit with the General he had been invited to travel to Riyadh to spend a day at the Equestrian Club. He jumped at the chance. This was surely a sign of his increasing favor with the military and also with the president and his cadre of advisors. In utter delight, he showered his family with gifts and discreetly bragged to his business associates. His bragging did not do justice for what was awaited him.

From the lobby to the ornate staircases, the large open spaces to the smaller private alcoves; from the tennis courts to the massage rooms; the facility had an ambience which was a feast for the eyes. It was on this day that al-Misri became all-powerful in his mind. Thoughts of his wife Hagar quickly receded in his mind. There was so much more to be had than what was the boring and steady diet of dutiful sex provided by his wife. She was as soft as a fig now. It was time to seek a new sexual partner; time for variety.

Within weeks of the birth of his sons, al-Misri rewarded his wife with a lavish home of her own in an upscale neighborhood in Cairo. He sold the home compound in Alexandria and purchased an ample love nest for his future conquests. With the family sorted out and hidden from view, he sought a suitable mistress.

Hagar loved the cosmopolitan feel of Cairo with its Parisian shadow. The streets boasted a large contingency of foreigners within the commercial district. The shops had more to offer and the streets were cleaner than those of Alexandria. Totally enthralled with the experience, she felt herself favored beyond her family counterparts. Increasingly, her focus was what her husband could provide. She had little thought to the man he had become. His largesse also spilled from her wallet to her parents and uterine relations. Al-Misri had recently instituted a monthly allowance for maintenance of the needs of the household. Hagar thought it was because her husband trusted her. The truth was a bit uglier. He just didn't want to be bothered by Hagar nor the children anymore.

Childhood memories can be selective. One of the most prominent of Hagar's early memories was from the first year of her elementary education. Her father had taken ill with a bad case of yellow jaundice. His eyes became fluorescent yellow and the scent of death was on his skin. He scratched constantly and his bed had been moved out onto the balcony to catch the occasional breezes which made their way onto the cobbled street. When she came to his bedside after school each day she was terrified to be near him and terrified to leave his side. Younger than the required age for such things, she would unroll his prayer mat and posture herself on it to pray to Allah, the Merciful, the Beneficient. Peeking through her hands as she prayed she watched her father as he dozed in restless manner. Occasionally, his hands would flail out toward the ceiling for no apparent reason. But mostly, she watched him scratch. He scratched and scratched his skin until it bled. Eventually he recovered and was restored to health. But Hagar never forgot the image of desperation which was presented by her father, and the reaction of the entire family to the hardship of those days. She remembers her mother saying, "We will never lack for rice, we will always find shelter from the rain. Beyond that, only Allah knows."

Because of this memory Hagar did not express sorrow when her father selected a man fifteen years her senior as her husband. Her mother's eyes gleamed when she spoke of the dowry. One day when she was in the kitchen she overheard her mother say to her father, "Of course it is because she is extremely beautiful. You must admit that the hair and the fine Egyptian features are because of me." With that she heard her mother laugh. She reflected that it was the first time she had heard the echo of her mother's laughter within the walls of the home in many months. Hagar reached into her pocket and pulled out a small round mirror. It was bi'dah (an innovation) and forbidden.

When it had fallen from the purse of a Western woman entering a taxi with her newly acquired purchases Hagar had quickly scooped it up and tucked it into the folds of her hijab. It was hardly big enough to show her entire facial features. Prior to that, she had to catch a glimpse of herself in a shop window. There was not a mirror in her family home. Now she hid in the courtyard as she pulled out the mirror. She examined her teeth. They were white and strong within her light brownish-pink lips. She pulled down her lower lip to take a look and stuck out her tongue. It had a velvet texture. Tipping the mirror up a bit she noted her straight nose, flawless olive skin and wide dark eyes under the umbrella of her eyebrows. For the first time in her life, she felt beautiful. Running her hands lightly across her breasts she knew that soon enough they would suckle the children of her husband. Beyond that thought she had little idea as to what awaited her in the marriage bed. Later that day she begged her mother to show her the small handful of photos kept in a crude wooden box under the bed. After becoming a scholar, her father had forbidden any further images of the family on film. But in examining the black and white pictures of her mother at a younger age, Hagar realized that what her mother had said was true. Her mother had also been a beautiful woman. Perhaps it was due to the fact that her own wedding day was approaching, but suddenly she felt a kinship with her mother which she had never felt before. And now – she would leave her mother for whatever awaited her, Insha'Allah.

At the beginning of the marriage al-Misri had seemed religiously devout. He attended daily prayers. A member of al-Ikhwan, he had performed the somewhat obligatory tour-of-duty in the parliamentary body. It had provided the beginning point for strengthened business and communal ties. But as weight of his presence in Alexandria increased, his shadow lengthened across the ecospace of the steel industry, and as the numerical value of his wealth began to rise he became seduced by the most common of mistress. Her name is power and the man with the mistress of power invariably ends with the standard ménage-a-trois. Power breeds corruption and corruption requires ruthlessness. Al-Misri became powerful, completely corrupt and utterly ruthless. Corruption is like a mouth full of bad teeth. Everyone feels the bite, but the most intimate of players, recognize the breath. It is a stinking and nauseating smell, one which can produce its own bilious response from the hypocritical pious.

Hagar initially remained in the dark regarding the true reason for the changes which were overtaking her husband. She loved the lifestyle he provided. No doubt about it. Her husband was kind to the girls and seemed to adore the boys when he would visit. But he had completely lost interest in her.   She felt invisible. He stayed out later and later at night and began to spend greater amounts of time in Alexandria. When he did spend the night with his family the interest in her did not extend beyond what she cooked for dinner. And the interest had turned to criticism. The fare was too plain, the meat not cooked to perfection, the bread not baked properly. He continued to assume a fatherly role with the children to assure that they were doing well in their studies. He would line them up at night and shout at them in rapid-fire manner asking questions about their grades and school companions. So Hagar brushed her concerns to the back of her mind.

She had become quite accustomed to creature comforts. The thought of a return to the constant menial duties which her mother and her sisters still performed appalled her. Her husband provided a car and a chauffeur should she and the children need to move about the city. She had only to call his office. Shortly, the ingratiatingly sweet receptionist would set up the service. The only shopping she did these days was to meet the personal needs of the family. Clothing her six children and parading them about the countryside had become her secret source of pride. The laundry woman scrubbed out their clothing on the cement rub board on the roof and hung them on a long clothesline to dry. If there was the least smudge on a clean item she promptly threw it back into the awaiting stack of dirty laundry. During the winter the woman's hands would crack and bleed. Hagar would buy her a jar of pomade at an area shop and feel benevolent for her act. The daughter of the laundry woman, a waif and pinched looking girl, would scour the marketplace choosing the best of garden produce for the family. She would eat a piece of fruit or munch on a carrot as she straggled along with her heavy woven basket. But she piously told her mother that she never stole from her mistress.

Hagar ventured into the halal butcher shop for the best cuts of meat. But little were the true labors for her household at this point. As is the manner of all wealthy women she became the manager of her home, an administrator of sorts, with a contingency of staff. So it was natural that as her leisure time increased, the subnormal level of any real activity gave her more time to spy on her husband when he was home. She had also gradually developed the possessive nature and profile of the scorned wife. The man she had married was the man she no longer recognized. She hated his hypocritical religiosity. The gifts he gave to the local imam and his grand display of zakat during Ramadan was a pompous display of generosity. The knife he wielded to cut the throat and sever the jugular of several fat goats to give a generous allowance of meat to the growing house staff was a sharp one. But as soon as Ramadan was over al-Misri would pull out a newly sharpened knife to use against his adversaries. In times past he had dealt kindly with his business associates. His business dealings had seemed honest. Hagar had quietly admired how her husband stepped into the bathroom with his left foot and out with the right. He put on his right shoe first and even combed the right side of his beard first. While doing so he would occasionally say, "He who gets his book of deeds in his right hand will go to Paradise, and he who receives it in his left hand will go to hell." Then he would smile pleasantly at himself in the mirror.

Now, she saw the underbelly of the man against whom her father constantly preached. Her husband was a hypocrite. Hagar felt intense shame in harboring the knowledge of some of her husband's actions. But more importantly, she was now beginning to physically fear the man whom she had loved and respected in the early days of their marriage. He never touched her in bed anymore. But she began to cling as closely as possible to the side of the bed which belonged to her. He made her skin crawl.

On three recent occasions al-Misri had placed secretive business calls from the Cairo home. Competitive business associates found themselves in jail on trumped up charges in less than twenty-four hours. Oh sure, the men were picked up and merely taken off the streets until al-Misri closed in on a business deal for which his associates had put forth all the time and effort. Granted, once the signature was dry on the contract and the first order placed with his company, the charges were mysteriously dropped. But the case which involved the third business associate tossed into jail was different. His wife was a friend of Hagar's cousin. Bad news travels fast in Egypt. The tale was of a dungeon-like cell deep within the security building basement. It was a dank and darkened space barely large enough in which to crouch. It contained one metal pot for a toilet and one enamel pitcher which was filled with water every morning. The story gave Hagar nightmares. The associate had been beaten viciously on his arrival and then lightly beaten for good measure on his departure. When her cousin whispered this news Hagar begged, "Please do not tell my parents. It will break their hearts." Her cousin hissed back at her, "You think a story like this will not reach their old ears?"

Although Hagar was not privy to the mechanics of the business dealings of her husband she learned the political trade of the boiler room by listening to the telephone calls he made on the nights when he slept in Cairo instead of Alexandria. Well-versed in the art of family intrigue – that interesting dynamic which accompanies extended households – she felt it her duty to keep her nostrils a bit flared for the smallest scent of news regarding her husband and his growing business empire. Nothing prepared her for the day when she overheard his conversation with his mistress. It was on that day that fear turned to intense hatred.

After Hagar learned that her husband's first mistress was ten years her junior she became more aggressive in fact-finding regarding her husband's activities. She carefully culled the daily newspapers which she would purchase from the area vendor. Seated on the pavement with his small rack beside him, the gummy-eyed illiterate would snake out his hand to receive his coin, and then invariably return to scratching his head lice. When her husband spent an increasing amount of time on the phone in the evening followed by 3-4 days of flurried business activity, she recognized his pattern. The story would be laid out in a day-by-day subplot, a simple few lines each day which did not expose her husband, but which confirmed the tale to which she was now becoming achingly familiar. Very carefully, she clipped and saved the articles in a box under the bed. She also assumed the role of a sentinel outside the bedroom as her husband sat on the edge of the bed to make a call to his mistress when he was staying in Cairo. And the greater her role as a spousal spy, the less her respect for her husband.

Khalid al-Misri picked up the telephone to hear the voice of Muhammad Qutb on the other end. After the usual pleasantries, enquiries regarding his family and business, Muhammad said, "I have a man here I would like for you to meet. May we send him to Cairo?

Will you host him and introduce him to a few of the brothers?"

Al-Misri responded, "Let me meet him first, but while accompanied by you. Perhaps we could meet at Janadriyah on Sunday. I have dabbled a bit in the camel races in the past and the track there is a good one. My jockey is young and proficient. Recently, a friend returned from the Sudan and spotted a camel clocked at nineteen kilometers an hour. He bought it on the spot. Although I am not yet in possession of Allah's best, I do have another sturdy camel with competitive edge." Qutb grunted in appreciation. Al-Misri continued, "It is rumored that King Fahd and members of the royal family will be in full attendance down to some of the youngest of children. Of course, I have had dinner with the king in the past. I also spent an afternoon engaged in falconry with one of his cousins last month. But back to the camel races and what to expect. Approximately three thousand camels are slated to race on that day. There will be dance troupes from Ta'if, al-Hasa, Yanbu'…" Qutb interrupted his tale, "Dancing is bi'dah. We are forbidden the dance." Khalid al-Misri responded, "The camel races then, a look at the work of the blacksmiths, examine the sawani and then we will enjoy a good dinner."

Sunday found al-Misri, Qutb and Dawud Malik engrossed in the camel races at Janadriyah. Thoroughly enjoying the races they took a mid-afternoon break at the invitation of one of the royal princes and reclined on large cushions within the coolness of the Bedouin tent and sucked on the glass stems of the water pipes. Platters of figs and sweet lemons from Cypress, goat cheese and an assortment of breads awaited them. In the distance they saw the cooking tents where it seemed hundreds of veiled women scurried about stirring pots, preparing the lavish platters of food for the men. The smell of garlic, saffron and cinnamon wafted in the air.

As the evening shadows moved across the desert floor the three men joined a circle of ten other men within a tent which accommodated a total of one thousand guests. There were dozens of such tents set up for the evening meal. Steaming platters of saffron rice with succulent portions of mutton were delivered to each group. Taking their right hand to pick a portion of mutton the men would then scoop with the index and middle fingers from the edges of the plate the portion of rice. Rolling a piece of mutton in the rice they would pop it into their mouths. Cool fruit water was served from large earthen jugs positioned nearby and the men were seated on cushions or their camel saddles. The rice and mutton were accompanied by smaller platters heaped with stuffed grape leaves, tahini, eggplant, and olives. Chickpeas and beans were served on smaller platters with garlands of lamb testicles around the edges of the platter.

After two hours trays began to appear with a variety of melons, figs, peaches and sticky cakes made with honey and nuts sprinkled with cinnamon.

It was when the stars blanketed the sky that Muhammad Qutb finally spoke what was on his mind.

1988

Dr. Dawud Malik, Ph.D stepped off the flight with a bedraggled wife, his two sons with sleepy eyes, and Aisha in rare form. His small daughter, a miniature of Maryam, sounded like a squall coming into the harbor. The flight had affected her ears and she was tugging at the right one as tears streamed down her face. Aisha had her mouth wide open and her uvula vibrated with her cries. She had also become separated from her favorite blanket after the last flight and was inconsolable. Maryam placed her hand over her mouth and told her to be quiet. Ibrahim and Basil were quiet and patient, like their father. Dawud smiled at his sons with fondness.

Making their way toward the first queue of passengers, the family was anxious to step outside the airport and into the fresh air. They would catch a cab and head to an area masjid. The local imam had agreed to host them for the night prior to their travel back to Deerborn.

The journey had been a nightmare of delays and their luggage had also disappeared into the great unknown. It meant there would be an additional delay as they were directed toward the courtesy desk to fill out a form for missing gear.

In spite of the hardship of the previous two days Dr. Malik had a confident step. He felt more clarity of purpose than at any time in the past. The building blocks of his training over the years had reached a mature threshold. He would take a month to get his family settled and then he would begin work as a Da'iyah. Never again, would he work in a secular field. His income would come from other sources. His specific emphasis on summer camps for Muslim youth was a given. To that end, he would set up a foundation and also begin an educational program which would provide educational materials to a network of mosques and Islamic education centers nationwide. But he was also full of ideas for future endeavors on behalf of his organization. Khalid al-Misri would subsidize his work with contributions to a charity which would funnel the funds into America via a "benefactor" awaiting in the shadows.

When he had last seen Khalid al-Misri, a neatly stacked bundle of American dollars had found its way into his hand.   Al-Misri said to him, "One of the allocations for zakat is to sustain the warrior. You are a warrior scholar. You are tasked with jihad of the pen and jihad of the tongue."   When arriving home, Dawud took his wife into their small bedroom and closed the door. He handed the money to his wife with a look of pride in his eyes. "I am just a faqir Muslim. What have I done to deserve such favor?" With trembling fingers, Maryam slowly counted the one hundred dollar bills twice. "Dawud," she said, "there is ten thousand dollars in this stack." Dawud took the money from his wife and then returned three bills into her outstretched palm. "Put this in your purse. When we arrive in Deerborn you will need to stock the food pantry for the children."

Maryam was both practical and frugal. The money was carefully guarded and not a penny was spent until arrival in Deerborn. She quickly located the best halal butcher, the finest local bakery and a nearby fruit stand which offered an assortment of seasonal gifts from the bounty of the earth.

With the assistance of the community Dr. Malik soon found space in a dingy apartment complex which was adjacent to a small park. Two swings, a slide and a sandbox did not count for much, but it would be sufficient for Aisha's needs. He had chosen the complex because it did not allow pets. Dawud had strictly warned his wife to beware of any dogs. His children had been warned regarding dog saliva. "Prophet Muhammad (PBUH) forbid us any dogs except for the hunt. From the looks of things the only things worth hunting are the squirrels in the trees, and we are doing the hunting of a different type," he said with a smile. Then picking up the phone he dialed the phone to speak with a contact living in Istanbul.

Ahmad as-Sirjani lived up to his name as a light-spreading lamp. But for those inside the ring of tarekat of the Naqshbandi he was also known as "The Architect". Classically trained in Islam with fluency in Arabic, and German he was rapidly gaining fluency in English. He was a Hanafi Sufi and his grasp of jurisprudence and capability for bringing the Qur'an to light had the crowds packing the mosques in Istanbul and beyond. Although not a scholar-in-residence, he was frequently called upon to deliver a Friday khutbah at any number of area mosques. Within the top circles of the Islamic society of Istanbul he was also noted for another gift – that of dream interpretation. His powerful influence had spread rapidly and in such great manner that now at the cusp of his fifth decade he found himself in great demand.

Presenting himself as a neutral and apolitical entity within the Turkish landscape he spent much of his time hidden away in his home meditating and writing books. Many of them were widely acclaimed, finding distribution paths across the world via the mosque networks. Yet he was not satisfied. Looking at the path along which his own schooling had taken him, as-Sirjani was acutely aware of the deficits of his own educational path and the manner in which he had to exert himself to receive his early education.

So it was, the Architect found himself seated with his good friend Dr. Muhammad Rahimullah, Ph.D on the balcony of his apartment in Istanbul on the day of Dr. Malik's call.

"What are your thoughts, Muhammad?" As-Sirjani offered up a quizzical gaze. Dr. Rahimullah looked at him quietly and put his fingertips together in contemplative manner. Both had been born in adjacent villages in 1939. Ahmad had the greater struggle when young. But a greater ability to acquire wealth had placed him far out ahead of his counterpart. While Dr. Rahimullah had established a large base of national support for his Da'iyah activities in the United States his friend had garnered an international audience.   Dr. Rahimullah took his place in life in stride. Meanwhile, as-Sirjani continued to amass financial wealth from his activities as a consultant for an international agency in need of human intelligence within Turkey's corridors of power.

Dr. Rahimullah knew that he should wish for his brother what he should wish for himself. But in this case the reverse was true - he also wished for himself the international recognition afforded his friend. He was fairly certain that Ahmad would never wish to be in his shoes. The squabbling masses of humanity which he had found within the mosque walls of the United States brought him little joy. The pettiness, backbiting and suspiciousness of their native and possibly tribal cultures were carried along their migratory paths like an extra piece of baggage. These characteristics were not left behind but imported with them. When the poorer immigrants touched the American shoreline they had little idea as to the difficulties which faced them.   They had hurdles transplanting themselves anew within the soil of the host nation. Many suffered from "back home syndrome" and could hardly wait to raise enough money to return home to view the misery which they had left behind. Raising funds for new mosques or new schools required a grueling travel itinerary and the stamina of an ox. As-Sirjani traveled a bit, but had the pleasure of the cloistered life of a prominent writer. When he traveled, the best hotels awaited him.   When Dr. Rahimullah traveled, he was invariably put up for the night by a Muslim family with five children in a three bedroom house.   He was given one of the bedrooms, but he always felt a bit guilty for displacing the children onto the living room couch or floor. At times his emotions moved to anger. Was he not worthy of a moderate hotel room of his own? He felt a bit of envy creeping into his psyche. He made a mental note to ask Allah's forgiveness later for the thoughts at the back of his mind.

So it was the two friends found themselves together again, the same as before, yet somehow vastly changed since their last meeting. The evening had progressed to include a formal dinner at one of the finer restaurants in Istanbul. Shared views with a few friends in common had provided for a delightful passage of time. "Afiyet olsun", the guests said to each other, at the end of the meal. All left via the side entrance provided for guests using the private dining area reserved for Istanbul's elite. Dr.

Rahimullah returned with Ahmad as-Sirjani to his home and they picked up a conversation thread where it had been left off at the time of the call from Dawud Malik.

When fielding the phone call from Dawud Malik there was little need for Ahmad to jot any notes. His ability to recall conversations in their entirety was well-known. Hence it was with a great deal of care that more than a few of his associates spoke with him. They were aware that their words might come ringing back into their ears anew years later. And their words would return with the same intonation, flash of the hands, or mannerisms which had been used. Great intellect is often accompanied by the tremendous gift of a carefully cultivated dry wit. As-Sirjani had a deeply drilled sense of humor within the bedrock of his intellect. Muhammad knew it well. But as they had been childhood friends there was never any sense of intimidation when in the presence of his brother. Now tipping back a bit in his chair, Dr. Rahimullah picked up the conversation as if there had never been a break in the thought.

"What do I think?" Muhammad paused for emphasis. "I think you should open a top flight Islamic school after your arrival in America. Make it such a stellar campus that our organization will fall all over its self to give you the funds for the second school. It must not present like the coinage of the Abyssinian dynasty. I have assisted in the fund-raising activities for seventy mosques in the U.S. now and a full quarter of them are expanded to include at least an elementary school facility. Out of that number ten of them are now in the process of expansion to provide education through high school. But a few of them are hardly worth the money which has been invested at this point. The Shura Councils still lack top talent and the communities do not throw their full weight behind the staff of the schools.

Dawud Malik will shortly enjoin the task of managing the flank of Muslim youth in America. He will provide summer camp opportunities to solidify their faith. We are at the beginning point of intensive summer sessions dedicated to Da'wah activities.

At some point, he will also be tasked to penetrate the federal prison system to identify the pool of disenfranchised black males to undergo Islamic training. We have examined this demographic and due to the vestiges of a matriarchal family structure from a post Civil War era they will find the patriarchy of Islam appealing to their manhood. The disenfranchisement which has come from the despicable history of slavery does not hurt our cause either.   Dawud will be an efficient operative. Eventually, we will expand operations to reach the incarcerated Hispanic male.   As such, the first transliteration of the Qur'an into the Spanish language is a work in progress."

"Won't it be quite a stretch to reach into the Hispanic population?" As-Sirjani looked steadily into the eyes of his colleague.   Dr. Rahimullah met the challenging gaze. "Of course it will be a challenge. But Allah's earth is spacious. And America is quite spacious when it comes to the accommodation of immigrants. The American missionaries dare not step onto Muslim soil. It is at the risk of their lives. But look at America. The nations mix and mingle. Are we not told that we are made into tribes so that we can get to know one another? Whether that tribe be Aztec or Zapotec, they move across the permeable southern border from day to day."

As Muhammad continued to talk, Ahmad was fully aware of the weight of rank of his dearest brother.   Dr. Rahimullah belonged to the World Council of Mosques in Makkah and was a yearly visiting professor at the Islamic University Al-Madina Al-Munawwara. So it was that both men secretly envied the other a bit, and that sentiment also fed their respect for the other.

Ahmad as-Sirjani kicked back onto the back two legs of his chair and propped his feet before responding. "It seems that I am suddenly gaining traction within the deep state apparatus. I have recently acquired a couple of valuable friendships within the military, and also am finding close alignment to my ideas within the corridors of the justice department. One man in particular, seems to be watching my back. I would like to see my writings receive a bit of a protected status, to see my thoughts introduced into the national school curriculum."

Dr. Rahimullah smiled tentatively and said, "Do you not consider the plan a bit bold? You are not exactly General Zia-ul-Haqq with the power of a nation at your disposal." As-Sirjani laughed softly. "General Zia-ul-Haqq may be dead but we both know his attempts at looking scholarly merely showed him to be the buffoon of Islam. He had the brain of a jackass clothed in a military uniform. He has destroyed the future of Pakistan, albeit the wretched citizens do not know it yet. His attempt to ideologically compromise the youth is no better a brown shirt effort than that attempted in Germany. I intend to bring the healthier ideological product to the school system. The normative values of Islam must be taught.

And in spite of Ataturk and his lengthy shadow, I will work my plan." His voice trailed off now.

Muhammad nodded with understanding. "Regardless, should you ever need to take flight and nest within my territory, let me know and I will take care of the details. Should you uproot from your pampered lifestyle in Istanbul, I will make sure that all arrangements are streamlined for your convenience." As-Sirjani looked at his friend with warmth and said, "I will never leave Istanbul. It is my home. And you expect me to give up my view of the Bosporous? I will die in Istanbul. My roots are firmly planted in the soil of the Ottoman Sultanate."

1997

By 1997 Dr. Malik had hosted multiple summer camp programs for high school Muslim youth. His favorite resource for the camps was "Towards Understanding Islam" by Abul A'la Mawdudi. Now in its sixth printing, it was fast becoming a favorite book for use in both the summer camps and also for the yearly Ramadan open house events being offered by area mosques. About 150 pages in length, it was concise and easy to read. Mawdudi had passed away in 1979. But as one of the primary architects of a contemporary Islamic resurgence his writings continued to surge in popularity. A passionate man, he founded Jamaat-e-Islaami in British India in 1941. In 1953 he clashed with the government of Pakistan when he sparked a riot against the Ahmadiyya community in Lahore. That gave him prison time, a death sentence which was later commuted, and the fame which accompanies such things. His tafsir of the Qur'an in the Urdu language, Tafhim ul-Qur'an (The Meaning of the Qur'an) was his most important work.

But during his lifetime he penned approximately 120 additional works and gave hundreds of speeches. His writings had a profound influence on the Indian subcontinent during his lifetime. And although his bones were laid to rest in an unmarked grave at his residence in Ichra, Lahore, the bones of his works still clatter about the world with regularity.

Dr. Malik revered the works of Mawdudi and also of Qutb. Perhaps it was not so much what was written on the page, but the pages of their life and history which spoke to him. He wished to pass this same level of passion on to his students.

He had created quite a following with his strong personality. He found his gift was Da'wah, the propagation of the message of Islam. With Maryman serving devotedly in the background, his reputation grew. He began to enter into a level of influence which moved him from a pawn to a knight on the geopolitical chessboard in North America. Securing an endowment through a philanthropic arm of the World Assembly of Muslim Youth (WAMY) he soon found himself in possession of a check issued on a bank in the Philippines. The money had actually traveled through an orphanage which functioned as a money-laundering front. The director would bring a busload of area children to the orphanage the day of the official visit from the government agency with oversight of child welfare. The children had a grand party, the bureaucrat and his two aides received a gift of cash for "a favorable audit", and village mothers got a day off. All would end well by five p.m. The director did keep a steady flow of children in and out of the orphanage for show, but none of them were truly orphaned. With the initial gift shunted his way from a benefactor in WAMY, Dr. Malik was able to start a small non-profit educational institute. He started with a board of directors of five. Three members were selected for him and he accepted them with good will. He insisted that Dr. Muhammad Rahimullah join the board as the fourth member and the choice was a good match. Dawud was the passion and Muhammad the patience; he was the zeal and his friend the wise counsel. A synergistic and beneficial relationship prevailed between them. The fifth board member was Ahmad as-Sirjani.

The newly established Al-Hakim Institute was initially hosted by an area masjid. Six months later, Dr. Malik set up shop in a large office space with a reception area at the front, his own office in the rear, and three cubicles on each side for a cadre of youthful volunteers. Initially his mission was to provide a plethora of pamphlets on Islam for his summer camps. A small local Muslim printing shop was secured for the task. Within a year, pamphlets were also being created for the federal prison project and a small army of male volunteers were being trained to proselyte non-Muslim men who had plenty of time on their hands and a world of resentment against the state.

Dr. Malik's activities were placing increasing demands on his time and personal assets. But beyond the daily routine of Da'wah activities was a world which he did not share with Maryam. It was a world in which only men were allowed. He was the newest initiate into the secretive organization which had administrative oversight for the continued protection of the hair of the Prophet Muhammad (PBUH). The Naqshbandi Sufi retained custodial stewardship. But possession of the pouch within these very capable hands was not considered sufficient. A network of international players stood ready to move at a moment's notice should any real threat materialize against their irreplaceable treasure.

Dr. Malik had been approached to join the organization while in Jeddah. It had been at the midpoint of his tutelage under Muhammad Qutb. The men had just finished praying in the open desert outside the city. Was not the earth considered a mosque and the sky a dome? Performing their ablution with sand they had bowed in rank as the voice of Muhammad Qutb rang out. As leader of the prayer he was a scholar in his own right. But it was the legendary shadow of his brother which gave him secondary political clout.

His manner was quiet and thoughtful as he approached Dr. Malik after the prayer. "Brother Dawud. We note the emergence of qualities of leadership within your character. It is the manner in which Abu Bakr was chosen. It is the manner in which our ancestors chose leaders from amongst themselves, and the manner in which we raise up our leadership today. I would like for you to join me in Janadriyah for the camel races. I have a man who has an interest in meeting you. He will pay all of your travel expenses. He will also donate money toward defraying the cost of your return to the United States when it is deemed you are ready to do your part for Islam in the Western hemisphere." Dawud looked at him with anticipation. "It is my honor to comply with whatever is requested of me." Muhammad Qutb gripped his shoulder firmly. "Good then. It is settled. Let us spend a bit of time within my tent enjoying a cup of tea." When Dawud left the tent that evening the shadows were playing across the landscape as if chased by the remaining rays of sunlight. Gold and amber mingled with bronze and umber. The sky appeared swollen with promise. The clouds held a promise of rain.

It had seemed to him the sky looked the same, today. Nature gave witness to the importance of the task. The Da'wah activities were critical. But the promise of a future surpassed the daily grind of his life.

The Architect

Ahmad as-Sirjani was seated on the deck of his home outside Falls Church, Virginia watching the lengthening shadows as they mixed with light and danced through the trees. It was the beginning of the winter season of 1997. He was feeling a bit melancholy regarding the recent upheaval within his life, the political atmosphere within Turkey which had forced his hand and caused him to pull up his roots from the soil of birth.

Misery catches its victims by surprise. And none was more miserable when the knock had come on his door six months earlier informing him that he had two choices. He could leave Istanbul or risk a lengthy enquiry into seditious activities against the government. His dearest friends suddenly became invisible. The few who would meet with him did not invite him to their home. Even their offices were off limits. He found himself reduced to standing on tree-lined streets to spend hurried and whispered moments seeking advice.

Every single one of his friends said the same thing. He must leave before the political heat became dangerous. The aide to a head of one of the federal ministries put it to him in the most succinct manner. "If you have a conference to attend abroad, now is a good time to travel a bit. Extend your stay. It will be good for your health." As-Sirjani left one week later. The landlord was tasked with shipping his library to Dr. Rahimullah. What remained, was to be liquidated and the funds given to the imam from his ancestral village.

He had thought Falls Church a wise choice. And it was proving to be so, with ready access to the vibrant Islamic network within the area. He had spent the first three months in the U.S. establishing and nurturing his American contacts. He then set out to arrange his library. Laying down Goethe's Das Ewing-Weibliche Zeicht uns hinan he felt intellectually satiated on multiple levels. His mind wandered to Al-Rahman, Al-Rahim and the Exordium of the Qur'an: In the Name of Allah, the Compassionate, the Merciful. Both were derived from the Arabic root rhm. The symbolic meaning of the root reminded him of this reading, albeit the primary meaning is the womb. He had somehow initially felt as if he was nurtured within a womb, with this move to America. The ayat were pregnant with meaning once again. The seven layers of the Qur'an were uncovered. He felt invigorated, excited, and ready for the task at hand. He had been the primary architect of the script and wordcraft for Islam in American in the decade spanning 1988-1997. Islam was to saturate the market as a household word, easy on the ear, yet of a neutral value. It was now time to unsheath his intellectual sword again for the decade-incremental goals for 1998-2007. As his thoughts journeyed between Turkey and the U.S. he became homesick. He was now firmly settled, yet unsettled in his spirit. Travel sprints would be restricted to within the continent and Western Europe. Within his own nation, he was a wanted man. But within the Islamic network of North America he was again the rising star which he had been in Istanbul. What a curse it had been that the city he so loved had been formerly known as Constantinople. What a curse, the dregs of Christianity which remained. And here in America, he found himself surrounded by populist Christians, a crazy patchwork of believers which he could scarcely understand and most certainly did not respect. Allah had not begotten a son. He was in the land of Dar al-Kufr.

He watched in silence. Snowflakes misted the landscape like miniature wings of Allah's angels. He slowly emerged from the mental cocoon, the place of annihilation which the Sufi knows full well. The butterfly must move near the flame.   And in the flame of annihilation he would emerge once again – the architect of a new decade. Qadaasa Allahu sirrah.

Hours later, Ahmad was still deep in thought, now inside his home with the fireplace popping and crackling with joy. Visualizing the deck which was now blanketed with snow his mind moved back in time to his relationship with Dr. Umar Rolf Ehrenfels. A statement stuck in his mind. "Individual philosophies create chaotic societies." The words rolled over again and again in his mind. It was true. Islam was the ultimate gestalt, the system of life by which mankind must learn to live. His thoughts now came to him like a lightning-quick flight. It was the sense of being on the back of Baraq, of making the night journey, in same manner as had been done in the seventh century.   His mind soared to the heavens. He willed himself to envision the written word of God, secured in heaven. He willed himself again to annihilation. Several hours later he opened his eyes. The house was completely dark, the fire completely extinguished. He rubbed his arms and even his bones felt the chill which had taken him unawares.

Universal Values. Two simple words. The vast application entered his mind. He was stunned by the simplicity and clearness of the command. He must craft a message of universal values. The words would sound secular, adaptable to the Western ear. But the cryptograph would be Qur'anic. Quite satisfied with this thought, he poured himself a cold cup of mint tea. Then he reached across his desk and placed a copy of the Constitution of the United States within his reach. It was time for a paradigm shift. And once the paradigm shifts, the way an individual interprets information changes. As-Sirjani allowed his mind to relax again and envisioned the duck-rabbit ambiguous image. The words of Thomas Kuhn came back to him, a passage he had memorized from "The Structure of Scientific Revolutions." Closing his eyes he envisioned the printed page in his mind.

"The subject of a gestalt demonstration knows that his perception has shifted because he can make it shift back and forth repeatedly while he holds the same book or piece of paper in his hands."

Time is really of no importance at all except to mark the affairs of men. The Sufi does not dwell within the temporal space, the finite timeline of history. There is no past, present or future. There are no cataclysmic events which necessitate a change in plans. God's plans are eternal. Sufism is not experienced. It is tasted. The Sufi eats less, sleeps less, and speaks less than others. There is little need to mingle with others. Ahmad as-Sirjani worked patiently for a month. The season continued to change around him. The days became shorter and the nights longer. The cold crept more steadily into the edges of the rooms of the home. He ate less but drank more tea. When he emerged again to view the world he had lost three kilos.

Satisfied with his work, Ahmad as-Sirjani picked up his phone and made a call to Dr. Jamil Nidal al-Filistini. He heard the lyrical voice of Dr. al-Filistini's wife on the other end. "This is Ahmad as-Sirjani. Would you please ask your husband to give me a call?"

That evening, Dr. al-Filistini returned the call. They discussed at length the concept of universal values. Dr. al-Filistini agreed that presenting the normative values of Islam which were compatible with the West was a good plan of action.

"Respected Ahmad", he said, "I have a proposal to make. It would be good for us to dispatch you on a lecture series within the mosque network to speak on universal values. Dr. Rahimullah has quite a strong network available. Allow him to be the point of contact with the area imam. I then propose that you also consider following through with a book of essays on the topic." As-Sirjani nodded vigorously in agreement, albeit with nobody in particular physically present to note his mannerisms.

His mind traveled back to Istanbul. He sorely missed the sound of the call to prayer. Someday ...in America.

Oasis

Dr. Dawud Malik's home was a watering hole. His years of conducting Muslim youth camps and the quarterly trips across the United States to speak at college campus conferences were paying good dividends. The recruitment of raw and youthful talent continued to go well. Working under the umbrella of the Muslim chaplaincy program within federal prisons, the rate of reverts to Islam was an enviable statistic. The black American males were the most malleable to the message of Islam. Disenfranchised due to their history, residing within a system of family units dependent on matriarchal strength, the message of strong manhood resonated well within their ears. Dr. Malik was also adept at feeding the parolee population into area masajid, assisting in finding employment for the men and also doing a bit of matchmaking on the side. The latter task could be tricky. Many sisters fled like startled birds if approached to marry a new Muslim.

A convert with a prison record and dubious educational level? But every now and then he would locate a wounded sparrow – either a widow, or a poorer sister in the masjid – willing to take the risk. Dr. Malik worked carefully to make the matches. Overall, the marriages ended up fairly successful. The selling point of marrying an American revert is that they did not have the wanderlust and proclivity to abandon the nest, as did some of the immigrant population. There were the men who would take off for the Hajj season and never return. Or there were the men who just disappeared without explanation who would reappear two years later to take their place in the home again. Dr. Malik's own marriage was strong. So it was hard for him to put up with the hypocrites who attended the mosque.

One of his recent goals was to secure funding for the printing of a Qur'an in Braille. He was teaching Qur'anic memorization to a young blind girl from his mosque and it brought tears to his eyes to see her struggle. But his greatest sense of accomplishment came from the Da'wah activities with young adult Muslims.

This particular evening he was seated in his living room with two of his favorite students. Zaid Langley came from an upper middle-class Protestant family. His father owned a large wheat ranch in Montana and Zaid was comfortable around both weapons and women. Dr. Malik was trying to mold his character regarding women and their rightful place in Islam. But he never touched the topic of the right to bear arms. Zaid's father had served back-to-back terms in the Montana State Legislature. He had strengthened the laws regarding weapons for personal use, and in particular, the sanctity of weapons used for hunting. Dr. Malik always reminded Zaid that Allah was the god of the hunt. His name was to be spoken over the arrow and also the hunting dog. It was to be spoken over the animal that was slaughtered. Zaid would agree enthusiastically. But it seemed that he was thoroughly in love with the concept of modern versus asymmetrical warfare. It seemed there was not a weapon that he couldn't handle. And he was an avid subscriber to several game and hunting magazines. Zaid was tall and thick like the trunk of a tree. He walked with the confidence of those with innate leadership qualities. And his laugh came from deep within the cavernous lungs, erupting with a sound which could be heard throughout the house. Maryam was quite fond of the young man. Whenever he had dinner with the family, she heaped his plate with portions equal to those of her husband. Then she usually added a bit more, smiling fondly at Dawud. "He is a growing boy! Look at the size of him!" Dawud would look at Zaid and think, "He is like the steed of Abu Bakr."

The second student present that evening was Uthman Goldstein. His father was the rabbi of a small synagogue in northern Maryland. Uthman sustained a counter revolutionary personality. Most likely his conversion to Islam was initially faked to get under the skin of his father. He was a man whom Uthman despised with an intensity which occasionally caught him off guard. When he was in high school, Uthman had found that his father was swinging from both sides of the plate. His father was a rabbi, a father of five children. The fact that he was also a cloistered homosexual who preyed on little boys destroyed the key relationship in Uthman's life. He told his mother what he had witnessed on the day he had come home from high school early because of a stomach virus. Although the details of what he had seen were graphic, his mother fell back on plausible deniability. "He was just horsing around with that child. There was nothing to it. You are imagining things." Uthman retorted angrily, "Since when does a young man prepare for his

Bar Mitzvah naked?" From the look in her eyes he knew that she knew the truth. But his mother flew at him in a rage and beat her fists against his chest. "How DARE you accuse your father in such a manner! You are a liar! A liar!" Damn her, if family social status was more important than confronting the family lie. He had been taught from religious texts which admonished the need for ethical behavior and personal integrity. As is the case in most families where religious instruction feels like the bones of a skeleton instead of the flesh of a living God, Uthman felt keen disappointment when witnessing the perversion of his father. The old man was a pedophile. The very man who had prepared him for his Bar Mitzvah, the man who had prayed side-by-side with him in Jerusalem was living a double life. Dear old Dad was a rabbi by day and a predator lurking in the shadows. Uthman maintained his relationship with his mother. But it was one born of pity rather than a relationship of love. Uthman had once read a quote by Oscar Wilde which seemed written for his family. "Children begin by loving their parents; after a time they judge them; rarely, if ever, do they forgive them." He could not forgive his mother for shielding his father from the consequences of his actions. And he could not forgive his father for raising him to believe in an ethical lifestyle whilst living his own life in a shadowed land of duplicity and lies. So when Uthman walked away from his Jewish faith he needed a place to land.   Christians on his campus prayed around the flagpole and had their little clubs. One of them had actually taunted him by saying, "Aren't you Jewish? Wasn't it your guys who crucified my guy?" But Islam reminded him of Judaism. There was structure and there was law. Two years after learning of his father's double life he was ready to embrace Islam.

Uthman was not initially accepted at the mosque he attended.   There was constant fear that he was a government plant, in spite of the fact he was only eighteen when he walked away from his Jewish heritage. But when Zaid Langley met him there was an instant bond.   The mildly effeminate Uthman found the role model he craved in his new friend, Zaid.

Zaid and Uthman were excitedly discussing the work of Sayyid Qutb with their mentor. Dr. Malik enjoyed his role as moderator. He was a muhadith, a scholar of Hadith. As the young men talked, he liberally added references from Hadith literature to what was discussed.

Zaid had veered off down a rabbit trail, as he was prone to do. Impetuous and intelligent, his mind was a rugged terrain of thoughts. He began speaking of the plight of Muslims in Chechnya. "The fall of the Soviet empire has opened a door of opportunity for ethnocentric political expression. But it is going badly for the Chechen Muslims. The dissolution of the USSR and balkanization of vulnerable populations had brought about a new handful of tiny nation states, some of which are rich in resources. But many of these regions are also damned by brackish religio-political waters which continued to clash against the vestiges of the Soviet state and her internal security apparatus." Zaid was really gearing up now, and it was to the point he forgot to swallow his spit. Dr. Malik noted a small trickle on the corner of his lips. It was a pattern with which Dr. Malik was becoming familiar. Zaid was increasingly passionate in his speech. He was looking beyond America and casting his gaze to the Ummah in other lands. Dr. Malik looked at Zaid and noted the animation in his features. Was now the time? Everything came down to proper timing.

Dr. Jamil al-Filisteeni had recently been in contact with him. He sought a few college-age Muslim men to travel to Gaza as part of a humanitarian effort. Zaid and Uthman seemed perfect. Adjusting his thaub a bit, Dr. Malik smiled at his two young guests. "Respected Zaid,

Chechnya is so far away and such a complex situation. But Palestine? The situation is not difficult at all. We could make arrangements. You and brother Uthman must travel to Palestine. You must see first hand the suffering of your brothers in Gaza.

The Jews stole the land. And the Europeans helped them to steal it, just to get rid of them. They were tired of the Jews, who (all of us know) can never be trusted. The whole world, is tired of the Jews. The day will come when the trees will cry out when a Jew hides behind them."

Sitting up a bit straighter and tugging thoughtfully on his beard, he continued. "Let me tell you about Dr. Jamil al-Filisteeni's grandfather. He lost his ten year old brother right before his very eyes. He was twelve years old when it happened. They had been kicking a ball and his brother went along the small ditch near the road to retrieve it. A car loaded with Jews left the road to run over him. He died on the way to the hospital. Dr. al-Filisteeni held him in his arms as he died. His grandfather's family was kicked out of their home near Jerusalem in the middle of the night. It was the Jews. They were given one hour to pack their belongings and leave. One hour, I tell you! And today? The Knesset sits on the land which belonged to Dr. al-Filisteeni's family. It is for that very reason that a small jar of soil sits on his desk to this day. It is the soil of the land stolen from his family. He still retains the keys to the family home. They are rusted. But they are the deed to the home, just as legal as the manner in which we use pen and paper to document a deed of ownership here."

Zaid and Uthman were leaning forward in their chairs now, intent on the story and engulfed in the action. "Dr. Jamil al-Filisteeni was actually born in a refugee camp set up for the Palestinians by the United Nations. His family never fully recovered their footing. He was born into an orphaned status, regarding his soil of birth. It is a miracle of Allah that he is successful today."

Zaid and Uthman were on the hook now. Dr. Malik just needed to reel them in. "Of course the brothers will help you to raise the funds. In fact, I will also contribute to your expenses. It is extremely important that Muslims in America understand the plight of their brothers in Palestine."

Later that evening, Dr. Malik called Dr. al-Filisteeni and reviewed his recruitment effort. They discussed the distinct beauty of sending young men to the refugee camps. Dr. Malik said, "We need to especially target Brother Zaid Langley. But perhaps we should caution him regarding discussing this venture with his father. He comes from a powerful ranching clan and his father still has strong political ties in Washington which extend beyond agricultural concerns." Dr. al-Filisteeni responded, "Send them my way. I will prep them for the next level of play."

Later that evening Dr. Malik lovingly caressed the books in his office. Running his fingers across the spines, each book represented an event in his life. Devoted to a sense of order for every aspect of life, he was fastidious regarding his library. Things were not alphabetized but were arranged according to his biographical timeline.

Indo-Pakistani have a cultural tradition, to let their children begin to read Qur'an at 444: fourth year of age, fourth month and fourth day. They have a celebration called Bismillah (in the name of Allah) with halwa /sweet and also additional food for guests. When little ones have completed reading the whole Qur'an, parents have another ceremony called Amin. The festivity also includes food. It is a joyous time of Islamic tradition for the Muslim community.

Dr. Malik's roots were Indo-Pakistani. So his parents had followed the tradition of 444 – allowing him to begin to read the Qur'an at the fourth year of age, fourth month and fourth day. He remembered the Bismillah celebration with the guests mainly being members of his family. But his greater recollection was of the Amin ceremony after he had read the whole Qur'an. He had read using the Juz system of reading. This Qur'an, was on the top shelf on the left hand side of the bookcase. But the Qur'an which had the most wear on the pages was the one used during Muslim youth camps. He taught the reading of the Qur'an using the Manazil method. The book was divided into seven Manazil, or stations. One station was to be recited each day. Dr. Malik would challenge the students. "Recite the complete Qur'an in one week after arriving home again. Then you must write me and tell me that my guidance has been heeded." In a box in the hall closet, were hundreds of letters from students who had risen to the challenge.

There was the work of poetry given to him at age nine by his paternal grandfather. It was the Rubaiyat of Omar Khayyam. For months he devoured the poetry of centuries past. He developed an insatiable appetite for knowledge. From poetry he progressed to the Seerah of Prophet Muhammad. By his early teens he was reading works of some of the early jurists of Islam. His family was not extremely well off but his mother recognized the gift of intellect within her son early in his life. She carefully skimmed small amounts from the grocery allowance to purchase books for Dawud. Within the pages of books, Dawud found a world which spread far beyond his limited childhood horizon. And it was these very books which spurred the young man to be the first in his family to migrate to the West to pursue his higher education.

Moving to the third shelf of the bookcase Dr. Malik located the picture books which were purchased from the streets of Amman, Jordan during his last visit. He piled several of them up in a stack. The next time Brother Zaid and Brother Uthman came to visit, he would introduce them to the geography of Palestine.

He felt a deep sense of contentment rise up within him. His wife was happy. The children were healthy. Islam was gaining ground in North America. Almost as soon as one mosque facility was completed, the ground for a new mosque was being laid elsewhere. Allah's earth was spacious.

2006

Dr. Jamil Nidal al-Filisteeni was a Palestinian electrical engineer who had done quite well for himself. As a consultant for global corporate projects in the Middle East, he had proved himself to be a highly valued asset. Based out of a tightly compacted office suite in Herndon, Virginia he also managed a PAC with a modest subsidy from Hamas. Sunni by birth and Hamas operative by choice he was one of Hamas most coveted agents along the eastern seaboard.

Several years prior he had actually met one of the top Hamas lieutenants in charge of operations. He was on a business trip to Syria and the scenario caught him completely by surprise. He was seated at one of the nicer restaurants in Damascus with a menu in his hand when he felt a tap on his shoulder. Looking up, he saw the man who had recruited and trained him. Somewhat startled, he rose from his seat and hugged him. "Abu Saad! What a pleasure!" Motioning toward the door, his friend escorted him to a waiting vehicle. An hour later, he was eating a simple meal of barley soup in the back room of a run-down, two table restaurant which had a chicken or two running in and out the door. The meeting was intense, and Dr. al-Filisteeni did not so much walk out the door a changed man; rather he walked out fully knowing the man he had become over the last few months. What had felt like a debriefing was in actuality a most intense new layer of indoctrination. His counterpart carefully guided his mind through a script which had been written long before he had been born. The oral and cultural traditions of the script had been learned on his mother's knee. Bits of the historical tradition had been learned during his elementary years. The military tradition had been instilled during the secretive meetings held after the Friday prayers. But now, the shards of information were carefully placed into focus. The kaleidoscope of history which dated from the time of the Sykes-Picot Agreement was shared over the meal. And when dessert was served, a look back in history was given to remind Dr. al-Filisteeni of the great loss which had been suffered by the Muslims of Palestine.

As he tossed in his bed that night, Jamil tried to remember word-for-word the conversation he had shared with a man he admired very much. The Palestinians had been victims for so long. But after two generations, the standard predator-victim paradigm no longer applied. The grandchildren of the victims were on the move politically.

A new class emerged. It could be a most dangerous class. The victimized predator can dish it out like no other.   Dr. al-Filisteeni was now mature on the stalk. He was highly educated. He was positioned for action. Everything finally came together in his mind. The Jews must pay. It didn't matter how long it took. The years ahead must become a grind of daily misery for Israel. When he returned he was no longer an engineer. That was just a hobby. That was a means to provide for his family. He was now fully and forever, a Hamas operative.

Jamil had a wife and two small daughters whom he loved. His wife worked as an assistant professor of mathematics at an area college and considered herself a progressive Muslim woman. It helped that her parents also lived with them and the extended family structure gave her generous time allowances to advance her own career. As for Dr. al-Filisteeni, his office staff consisted of a secretary and receptionist, and shadow staff in the form of a Palestinian graduate student working on his law degree at Georgetown University.   Khalid al-Nur was young, ambitious and completely devoted to Dr. al-

Filisteeni. They had grown up within two blocks of each other in Gaza. Khalid remembered the time when Jamil taught him to bounce the soccer ball off his head to then catch it on his heel before kicking a goal. Khalid was about six years of age at the time and the fact that a teen-age boy would pay attention to him greatly impressed him. His friend was already sporting the patchy stubble of a beard as noted in adolescent boys who are at the beginning point of the hair distribution map of their bodies. That also impressed Khalid and he would self-consciously stroke his smooth cheeks whenever he headed home after a game of soccer with his friend. He became Jamil's sidekick. The elder of the two took on the mentorship of the younger. The physical dexterity which both men exhibited in their younger years matured to include a mental dexterity and cagey intelligence which made them a formidable team. Dr. al-Filisteeni requested that Hamas sponsor the Western education of Khalid and the investment was beginning to pay off. Hamas was impressed with the quality of Khalid's nascent spycraft and paid him liberally for his snippets of information. His usefulness as a regional courier was also duly noted. As Khalid was in the top two percentile of his class he found his stride making the circuit of the many lectures, symposiums and conferences which were offered. As often as possible he turned the conversations toward international law and the plight of the Palestinian people. Careful to never speak against the state of Israel and particularly diligent to never utter the word "Jew" he carefully moved through the minefields of conversation. He analyzed trends and possible policy nuances which might affect Hamas. He probed gently for attitudinal shifts of his professional peers. He profiled every person he met and built a substantial dossier on any person of interest, when requested by Dr. al-Filisteeni. By the time he graduated from Georgetown, he had unusual grasp for the political climate of the Beltway and an absolutely enviable contact list.

Dr. al-Filisteeni also attended many cocktail receptions and was a darling of the political left. Lauded as a moderate Muslim with a PAC involved in political mediation for Muslims he was on the precedence list for many of the parties held by Washington's elite. He had gained the expertise of holding a cocktail in one hand whilst never taking a sip throughout the evening. Every intoxicant is khamr so every intoxicant is haraam. He extended the line of thinking via laws derived from Qiyaas. Thus it was, that he was also in agreement with the Muslim scholars and the ruling they made when tobacco reached the Ottoman Empire in the 17th century. Smoking was Makrooh (disliked) and smokers' breath was no better than garlic on the breath in the mosque. Occasionally, he would be seen eating at these events but for the most part he satiated himself with the latest chatter. If he did eat, it was the oceanic selection.

Inside the Beltway it can be the little things which count when writing up the monthly report which is hand-delivered to leadership in Gaza which then travels to the leadership living in Syria. Once a month he would call the small janitorial service which cleaned his office space and complain of a streaked window, lack of toiletry supplies or something small. That evening, Khalid would make his way to a restaurant which served halal food and the information would be passed along. The courier on the receiving end was constantly rotated but Khalid was the unchanging variable. There had been no signs of surveillance and it was extremely infrequent for a non-Muslim to enter the small restaurant situated four blocks from the metro station. When the wayward customer inadvertently stumbled into the space they were treated politely, served their meal within 2-3 minutes, the waitress would take their plate taken away with the last bite still on the fork, and the message was usually received at least on a subliminal level. This was a Muslim neighborhood restaurant. Outsiders were unwelcome.

The timely intelligence successes for the organization were being noted at the highest levels. Jamil and Khalid's combined uncanny sense of the operational tempo within Washington had kept Hamas from being blindsided on multiple occasions. With the Neocons controlling the political landscape things were a bit harder, but the challenge of penetrating the political power grid did little to dampen the enthusiasm of area Hamas operatives.

CAIR was suffering a public image problem. The online signature petition "Not in the Name of Islam" had fallen a bit flat. Every scent hound within the anti-jihad industry was hot on their tail, and their numbers were dwindling. Any reinvention, reincarnation or resurrection within Washington was amply appreciated. Dr. al-Filisteeni and in particular, Khalid al-Nur, were the fresh faces on the political scene. Missions never change. Only the players on the stage are new.

Also within Dr. al-Filisteeni's network was Bilal Stephens PhD., a man with whom he shared his deepest thoughts. He was eldest son of a Baptist minister. His mother managed the children's department at the church. The man formerly known by the name of James Stephens had never really embraced Christianity. He had made what he felt was a forced and obligatory confession of faith. It was followed by a very public water baptism on Palm Sunday with his own father performing the rite. He had always resented that moment in time. His adversarial relationship with his father caused him to see his baptism as just one more act of domination by a man for whom he had intense disrespect. Also, he just couldn't see the point of a man on the cross with an open display of weakness, going down without a fight. After his baptism he made his way to the parking lot to puncture one of his father's tires with a pocket knife which he had carried along for the occasion. Later filled with remorse, James Stephens assumed the role of a good Christian son until he left home for a university education.

When approached by the Muslim Student Association to attend an informational meeting, Stephens was initially ambivalent. Having lived a lie regarding his Christian faith he was not keen on what had the scent of indoctrination. But somehow he found himself coming back to the meetings again and again. He moved into a crash course of reading the Qur'an followed by instruction on the life of Prophet Muhammad given within the cramped office of the professor who chaired the Islamic Studies Department of his university. Reading about the Muslim spiritual leader he found a man whom he could follow. No "turn the other cheek" for him. About the time he finished a course of study on the Ghazwats of Prophet Muhammad he gave witness and changed his name to Bilal, to honor the Abyssinian slave whom Abu Bakr had set free; a man who later became the first muezzin of the nascent Islamic state. Instructed by the professor to return home and perform Ghusl, Bilal felt like a new man, one given a purpose and destiny in life. As a black American male who had felt disenfranchised from his father, scorned by white people and never quite coming to grips with his own masculinity, Islam gave him comfort. He suddenly found the identity which he lacked. "I am a Muslim." He looked in the mirror as he said it and it gave such a sense of affirmation that he said it again. "I am a Muslim!" Bilal embraced his new identity with fervor. And on his first trip home after conversion, he announced the news right before the Christian prayer for a Thanksgiving meal. Firmly grabbed from behind by both of his elbows he found himself thrown onto the front lawn by two of his male cousins. The last sound he heard as the door thudded shut behind him was the shrieks of his mother and a string of curse words from his father.

Bilal dropped his plans to become a psychiatrist. Financial donors mysteriously appeared and Bilal eventually found himself living in Riyadh and pursuing a Master of Arts in Islamic theology. He was subsequently funded to pursue his doctorate in Islamic studies at the University of Wales.

Dr. Stephens moved to St. Louis, Missouri in 1995 to head a new masjid situated within the inner city. Dr. Jamil al-Filisteeni was present at the masjid for his installation as the new imam. Within months, Jamil became the primary influence in Bilal's life. He carefully cultivated his new friend. Bilal moved from being a moderate Muslim to a radicalized anti-West imam.

Marie Claire

Marie Claire. Marie Claire Simon. Khalid rolled the words around on his tongue again and again. As he thought of Marie Claire his tongue tasted her skin, and he remembered her perfume. In his mind, he saw her image. It was never with the stylish clothing from a well-maintained wardrobe. She was always naked, and even when not present, his mind was constantly being seduced with thoughts of her.

Life had remained much the same since joining Dr. Filisteeni as legal counsel for the political action committee. A newly-established charity functioned as a front for the necessary money laundering. This took Khalid away from the world of spying and he was instructed to administrate his various duties and keep his nose clean. He was also tasked with building a personal network for future exploitation. But there was to be no actionable information gathering activities. He was to focus on NGO's and private organizations and donors with any level of interest in the Palestinian cause. The pot of money was diminishing by the day with regard to support from the Muslim community in North America. Everyone was jittery. The men especially, felt themselves to be under a shadow of surveillance.

Khalid's daily routine had become pathetically redundant until the day he had met Marie Claire at a regional rally in support of the Palestinians. When she walked past him and he caught the drift of her perfume he was interested. But well aware of the danger of olfactory stimulants he purposefully moved a few paces away. But when she had dropped her sign in front of him and bent over to pick it up he was hooked. She had a remarkable set of legs and what sat on top of them interested him even more. His testosterone took over and within two weeks his pious celibacy was a thing of the past.   Of course he could say nothing of this transgression within his community of friends. But Khalid acknowledged the truth to himself as he looked into the mirror every morning. The woman had her hooks in him and at this point he didn't give a damn.

For her part, Marie Claire had been very careful to position herself near Khalid at the beginning of the street rally nearly four months earlier. In a matter of days she had fully acquired her target. She had his body. Now she started the patient and painstaking work of owning his mind. As a person of interest, her role with Khalid took familiar form: seduce and juice. Pick the fruit, and squeeze it for every last bit of information. When the last little bit of useful information had been extracted she would disappear. There would be a new job assignment in an obscure location. There would be the invention of a pregnancy and abortion. It would be followed by an angry letter. Khalid would experience both the guilt and the luck which can accompany escaping a failed relationship. Marie Claire would make sure of it.

Normally, there was a six month operating window for female operatives assigned to men on his level of activity. Only government leaders within high ministerial or cabinet level positions were afforded the operative who functioned as a long term mistress. The training track was different, because of the greater sensitivities of the assignment. The majority of these men had wives and children. Handlers for these women mainly worked to assure that the anonymity of contact was not breached.

For reasons which she could not quite define, Marie Claire was actually enjoying this lower level assignment on a companionable level. Khalid was an avid sports fan and presented publicly as a prototype alpha male. Marie Claire had played sports all of her life and was an avid fan of any event which pitted man-against-man. Khalid also had an intellectual side. His library was stocked with many notable memoirs, historical selections and the poetry of Rumi and Omar Khayyam found place with works by Shakespeare, Abraham Lincoln and Nietzsche. The trappings of his Western education were apparent and yet in private he was also the picture of tremendous religious restraint. He prayed Surah al-Fatiha seventeen times a day. He observed the daily prayers. And he held to a halal dietary menu.

His ability to compartmentalize his sexuality apart from his religious identity was something which Marie Claire did not quite grasp. Marie Claire would bait him with the topic of marriage and use it as a can opener to explore his vulnerabilities. He would sleep with her but he would not marry her. He had told her already that it would break his father's heart. "Sure," said Khalid, "I am allowed to marry a woman who is from the People of the Book. But you have not met my family!"

Khalid and Marie Claire were seated at a small restaurant which had a halal certificate proudly displayed on the wall. The owner was from Pakistan and his brother was the cook. The brother's wife was the only waitress and most of the business came from a trickle of foot traffic from an adjacent apartment complex which was largely populated by immigrants from the Indian subcontinent. The menu was a mix of Persian and Indian style cuisine, so the menu offered a mix of both spicy and mild selections. Khalid usually ordered the hottest of curry selections. Marie Claire would content herself with a platter of grilled meat which included "signature kebabs" made of succulent lamb. Finishing their meal, they walked hand in hand to Marie Claire's condominium. Khalid was in the mood for a bit of action. On this particular day, Marie Claire was preoccupied but she would lay aside the worry from the phone call she had received when Khalid was paying the check. Her mother had just received a diagnosis of breast cancer. Her sister had called to gently deliver the news to her. So she masked her anxiety and smiled brightly at Khalid when he asked her if he might spend the night with her.

Because of her anxiety regarding her mother, Marie Claire did not process the significance of the last bit of information she had received from Khalid as she playfully ran her hand across his body and said to him, "Khalid! You have one premature grey hair on your chest!"

Laughing, he raised up on one arm and looked into Marie Claire's grey eyes flecked with emerald green. "Yes, I do! But the more important thing is that I know the location of the hair of Prophet Muhammad (PBUH)!"

Sending her weekly report off via courier the following morning, Marie Claire did not mention the hair of Prophet Muhammad. She duly noted the information regarding the house on Leicester Square.

The normal length of time which her organization allowed a female operative with a target like Khalid was six months. Marie was counting the weeks until she would be allowed the three months at home base and then a return to the field and a new assignment. She was already experiencing the ennui which accompanies the third assignment. Her handler was aware of the statistics. Most women were good for 3-5 assignments and then they bolted. They wanted to settle down with a nice Jewish husband and put their productive organs to use. If the agency was lucky, they could entice a short-termer to the longer term career track as a faithful mistress. The odds were about 1 in 20.

Two days after filing her weekly report Marie Claire found herself suddenly whisked to the airport to board a flight to Tel Aviv. She assumed it was the news she had delivered regarding the house on Leicester Square. Khalid had been her third target in less than two years, but this was the first time she had been ordered to return to home base prior to filing a final report. The agent who stood stiff and unsmiling at the door to her condominium asked her to grab a pre-packed suitcase with the few essentials necessary for rapid flight. This was the first time she had found it necessary to remove the bag from the closet of the spare bedroom. The agent hissed into her ear, "A team will be sent in shortly to deal with any remaining evidence of your existence." He handed her a new passport and told her that she would be met at the gate in Tel Aviv. "Sleep well on the flight, because you can expect several hours of debriefing on your arrival home." Yuri Cohen gave a tight little smile and then he was gone.

Marie Claire did sleep for a good portion of the flight because she was afforded the stretching room in the first class cabin and also had the presence of mind to take an Ambien almost immediately after take-off. The action was strictly forbidden, but her nerves were in such bad shape that she felt she needed the rest. She remembered being told in her training how upper level operatives were not allowed to move from surgery to the post anesthesia care unit without a minder of sorts, to keep them from blurting out state secrets whilst still under the influence of anesthetic agents and a cocktail of narcotics and benzodiazepines. She had endured an emergency appendectomy six weeks earlier, and obviously, had not warranted such special treatment. When she awakened more fully in the Day Surgery Unit it was only the next door neighbor and Khalid who stood at her bedside.

She gave a wistful, hidden smile as she remembered the last time she had set foot on Israeli soil. She had grown up in Tel Aviv. And yet she felt she had walked every mile of coastline, every hill and valley, during her childhood and young adulthood. As she began to doze off she remembered what she had overheard the day before leaving for her current assignment.

"Marie Claire is as competent a whore-for-hire as any of them." She had heard the words as she walked toward the open door of her boss. Immediately incensed she had a flash of anger which desired confrontation. But she was too driven to succeed to do anything which might cause him to blackball her or pass her over for a desirable assignment. And later in the day when she was briefed regarding her target, all was forgiven. So it was that she moved from sleeping with a mid-level bureaucrat from the intelligence bureau in Alexandria, Egypt to being sent to Washington, D.C. She had learned to take the good with the bad. Her fluency in Arabic from summers spent in Morocco certainly helped. Her breeding, education and looks made her valuable within the field of intelligence gathering. Men will always share more openly with a woman they consider an intellectual peer.

An hour before the aircraft landed Elise awakened to the sound of the pilot giving the latest weather report. Taking a few moments to refresh her make-up she requested a glass of white wine. What awaited her, of that she was unsure. But it was this very mystery which was causing her stomach to lurch a bit.

Arriving at Ben Gurion Airport, Marie Claire was spotted by her contact and he flashed a badge. Leading her to a private corridor they bypassed immigration and normal customs procedures. Exiting the airport they were greeted by a gray sedan. Opening the back passenger door Marie took her place and the escort seated himself in the front with the driver. The highway took them eastward toward flat landscape covered with shades of green and then they began to climb bit by bit the backbone of the mountainous road which led to the city of Jerusalem. They passed places which stirred her memory bank: Rehovot, Ashdod and Beersheba, and villages along the road. She could see children kicking about a soccer ball in the distance and the air smelled crisp and pure compared to that of D.C. Entering Jerusalem the driver sped toward King Saul Street and the meeting which Marie Claire knew awaited her. Digging in her purse she located a breath mint.

Striding up the stairs to the second floor Marie Claire was placed in a Level II interrogation room. She knew the drill for she had been the observer as opposed to the observed on several different occasions when dealing with female prisoners of note. Her every word would be recorded, undoubtedly a few of her colleagues would be on the other side of the mirror to enjoy the show. The video capabilities were of such high quality they would record any first bead of sweat which showed on her brow, even the smallest flicker of fear in her eye.

There were at least two other female operatives who had been disappointed when not handed the dossier on Khalid al-Nur. One of them had called her a "one trick bitch". But as they were also on the same assignment rotation it was unlikely they would be present. That thought gave her a momentary sense of peace. But it was the man seated at the opposite end of the table which gave her ample   reason for panic. She was still unaware as to the reason for such a sudden flight home. Her last report had seemed routine enough. Her companions in the sedan had ignored her on the return to Jerusaelm. But the man seated on the other side of the table was a legend in the intelligence community.

Col. Ari Barak had a boyish appearance for his age. But it was his operational capacity for ruthlessness without leaving a discernible trail which now placed him as the second in command of his agency. The word "early promote" comes readily to mind. Although he had officially retired from the military eight years prior, his legendary tactical prowess caused his rank to follow him within the halls of Israel's top intelligence-gathering apparatus. His genius was in operational planning and state sanctioned executions. Only a fool with a death wish would have considered addressing him as anything other than Col. Ari Barak. Few were the men comfortable enough in his presence to address him in a casual manner. His wife even referred to him as "the Colonel" when speaking to her closest friends.

The last known operational action of Col. Barak of which Marie Claire had been aware was told to her in a whisper. It was the assassination of an elderly retired Russian statesman who lived in a small fishing lodge along the Baltic Sea. It mattered not that he now survived on a small pension and spent his days reading, fishing, and playing cards with a couple of friends. Little need to consider that dental records now showed the sign of decaying teeth of the near dead or that his last chest x-ray had shown mild cardiomegaly. He must have his skull cracked in the same manner that he had cracked the skulls of the last five Jewish boys who had been "spared" to drag the bodies of the other children from the back of a truck to their awaiting trench grave in the forest. The one Jewish lad who had survived the rifle butt to his skull had managed to make it to Israel after the Soviet Empire crumbled. As an elderly Jew, the story was just another tale from the kaleidoscope of Jewish history during the holocaust. But in his case, he had put to memory the coordinates from the map which was carelessly tossed atop the fresh dirt of the burial site. His story circulated and was believable enough that the tale soon found its way into the security apparatus.   An excavation team was furtively dispatched under the guise of international scholarship. The images they sent back via satellite pierced the hardest of Israeli hides.

Some of the skeletal remains were of babies. The survivor estimated assisting in dragging thirty bodies to the trench. Possibly due to the psychological trauma he seemed unaware of the nearby trenches already covered with fresh dirt. The low end of the estimate of Jewish remains was two hundred children. Bone measurements determined that most of them were under the age of eight.   The carefully collected story of their manner of death had emerged after several months of a forensic historical search. The children had been roped together "so as not to waste one good bullet on young Jewish scum", as noted in the personal diary of a participant. Col. Ari Barak had insisted on leading the team in spite of the tremendous risk. And from his first act of bravery on behalf of his nation until his final known operational act which was accomplished in the prior decade, there were few who loved Col. Ari Barak. But across the board everyone feared him on some level.   His predatory instincts did not fail him as he cracked the skull of an elderly Russian man as he sat on a pier with his fishing pole beside him. Colonel Barak calmly drank from the whiskey flask on the small table beside his victim, swabbed the inside of the man's cheek for a DNA sample, and then tossed the body into an awaiting vehicle which sped the remains to a nearby crematorium. As Marie Claire seated herself across from Col. Barak she saw the eyes of a wolf. Deadly calm.

Col. Barak was not one to waste words. Every second counted for the security needs of his nation. He even had a well-known mannerism of saying "Every second counts," while running his fingers through his hair. Only his wife knew the truth regarding his mannerism. As a child of eight years he had been called from his school classroom and informed that his father was dying. The family had struggled as the the patriarch moved rapidly toward death at the hands of pancreatic cancer. For some unknown reason, Ari had taken the time to walk the long hallway to the bathroom and carefully comb his hair. It seemed important to look presentable for his father. Then racing to his bicycle he pedaled home in furious manner. When he stepped across the threshold of his home his uncle stood waiting for him. Putting a firm hand on his shoulder he spoke words which break a heart. "Ari Jacob Barak, your father died just one minute ago. His last words were to speak your name." As the firstborn son and the sign of his father's first strength, Ari was besieged with a sense of overwhelming guilt. He began to drive himself toward achievement in school, sports and even in pursuit of girls. He became ruthless with himself and eventually ruthless with others. Men under his command within the intelligence branch of Special Forces would crouch in predatory manner waiting for him to run his fingers through his hair and say, "Every second counts!" This was their signal to leap into action and execute a plan. His men considered him unstoppable. Yet the officer-in-charge knew the truth. He had stopped to comb his hair and missed the final moments with a man whom he fiercely loved.

"Every second counts!" Col. Ari Barak looked across the table at Marie Claire with eyes which were neither grey nor blue; brown nor black. The iris were the color of steel. Without looking at the open report on the table he ran his fingers lightly through his hair and then tapped his middle finger rapidly on the table almost as if delivering a burst of Morse code.

"We followed up on the anecdotal information regarding Harut and Marut being tied together and hanging upside down in a well in Babylon. We have heard this tale before. And in all honesty, if we could find them and cut them loose to teach their black arts again we would recruit them for the agency. We would pay top dollar to employ them. We have our own foul renegade angels and what is two more." He paused to light a cigarette. "But the anecdote regarding the hair of Muhammad is one which we have heard only once before, and it was spit out by a Palestinian whom one of our soldiers had knocked practically senseless in the basement interrogation area. We all know that the cloak being waved around by Mullah Omar in Afghanistan is pure showmanship. The cloth comes from a village in Yemen. We have even interviewed the kat-chewing hag on whose loom it was woven. But should there truly be the hair of Muhammad safely secured in Hyderabad we need to lay claim to it as it is a trophy of incomparable value."

As Col. Barak talked Marie Claire felt the blood drain completely out of her face. The wolf noticed and circled closely. "What? You are surprised that we heard every word spoken in your bedroom, that we practically smelled your sweat as you slept with the enemy? We do take care of our people. You are an asset. A bit on the thin side, I might add." Marie Claire had the sensation of floating. She could care less if he had seen her in action. But she had noted that he did not use the adjective "valuable" with the word asset. He almost said it as a curse.   She felt her knees begin to grind together underneath the table. Preparing herself for the worst she forced herself to relax her fingers.

Col. Barak glanced at the door and Yuri Cohen entered to take a seat beside the Colonel.   With a completely impassive face and a voice almost completely devoid of inflection, he said, "Tell us everything you know."

Marie Claire recounted the story twenty times. "Yes," said Yuri, "We are aware of the Science of Hadith and the subdiscipline of Shamail. We have a copy of "Shamil al-Tirmizi" by Abu Esa Muhammad al Tirmidhi translated in both Hebrew and English in our archives.   We confirmed the standard 'fourteen gray hairs' of the Prophet.   What we lack is the current location for the pouch holding the product. Khalid stated it was moved from the Balkans to Hyderabad during the effort at cleansing the landscape of the Sufi influence? He stated they are now at the home of a Sufi in Hyderabad? The place is a maze of streets and a labyrinth which boggles the mind. Yet he did give indication of adjacent structures, did he not? And he had tea with the owner of the pouch?   Marie Claire nodded slowly.   Both men stood up abruptly.

Col. Barak glanced at the operative who now had the appearance of a cornered animal. There was no malice in what had been done. An interrogation is an interrogation. It had been handled professionally and every psychological maneuver possible had been used to elicit any further information useful to the team which was ready to move forward with this most sensitive operation. "You will leave immediately by helicopter for Hatsim Air Base. The staff has pulled some maps which you may find interesting. A light meal will be provided for you during the flight." With that, the door opened and Marie Claire was escorted to an awaiting vehicle.

Col. Barak drummed his fingers on the table and Yuri thought it had the cadence of a forced march.

Khalid al-Nur

Khalid stood at the door of Marie Claire's condominium and pressed the buzzer again and again. The place looked dark and he had not seen her vehicle in the designated parking spot. Fingering her business card he remembered the day she had handed it to him and somehow without thought he had looked at it and placed it in his wallet. As he flipped it back and forth on his palm he realized that the paper stock didn't seem right and it was too light a paper weight for her title as a Vice President for International Product Development of a noted firm in France. But more than anything else he remembered the time when she had taken a call on her cell phone and he overheard her refer to the caller as "Esther". She later told him the call was from her sister. Esther.... Esther.... Esther... He gave a small involuntary shudder. He remembered what his Hamas contact had told him the first time he had delivered a packet of information after attending a soiree which was hosted by an ambitious and cocky Congressional aide. "Remember Khalid, there is always a Jew in every palace. And in this particular palace, there are many Jews. There are AIPAC Jews, there are banking Jews, there are spying Jews. If you drive along the streets with multi-million dollar homes, you are in the neighborhood of the Jews. If you attend a function, you are eating under the sponsorship of a Jew. If you walk inside the banks the Jew is reaching into your pocket. There are only two cities on the planet where you can walk and not be in the presence of a Jew; and only one strip of land on the planet where the Jews are actively resisted with the blood of our children. It is our beloved Palestine." With this, his contact gave a self-satisfied look.

Khalid then remembered a recurring dream he had for three nights in a row the prior week. In the dream a woman with her facial features blurred would open the door to a large clay oven and beckon Khalid to walk into the fire. Khalid would always resist and the dream would end. He would awaken with sweat on his body and ponder the symbolism of the dream. He knew it would have been good to take the dream to his imam for interpretation. But in his heart the truth was there. Marie Claire was the blurred face in the dream.

Patiently, Khalid al-Nur performed the ablution for the Friday prayer. Already he had brushed his teeth with a traditional siwaak on the drive to the mosque. After wiping his hair and beard, and cleaning his ears, he placed a handful of water in his right hand, gargled, and spat it out. He inhaled a small amount of water into his nostrils and expelled it with the left hand. He did this three times. After washing his upper extremities three times he proceeded to clean his lower extremities. He washed his right foot up to the ankle and his left foot last. The persistent triad of tradition caused him to remember again certain elements of his dream. The clay oven had three tongues of fire.

When wiping his head, his beard and then cleaning his ears he had already purposed that he would speak to Dr. al-Filisteeni on Monday morning. Hurrying along, he prepared to bow in rank with his brothers. Looking around, he thought he saw the jinn on either side of him.

Khalid returned to his residence late in the evening. Deep in thought, he did not notice that the Himalaya salt lamp which cast an eternal glow from the front window was not on. When he closed the door he felt a hand across his mouth. As the knife slid across his throat the words, "Forgive me, my brother," were whispered into his ear. Seconds later, he was dead.

Triple Play

Khalid al-Misri was seated in the living room with a glum look on his face. The television was blaring in the background but al-Misri was deep in thought. As was his manner when deeply worried, he was pinching his nostrils together as he leaned on one elbow.

Things were not going well for him on the home front. His eldest daughter was openly rebelling against his authority. It necessitated his return to Cairo more frequently than usual. He was near to his breaking point for patient response and had discreetly enquired into the fees for a boarding school in Scotland. It was a small and secluded ladies-only campus and the only male within twenty miles was the headmaster, who was well-known for his strict rules and swift punishment when challenged.

Hagar was complaining about her household budget and constantly asking him for an increase in the monthly allowance. But he had held tightly to his wallet. He knew that she was helping her parents. That expense, he did

not mind. Allah commanded that we care for our parents.
But he had recently discovered that she was funneling
money to a cousin whose husband was both a drinker
and a gambler. Al-Misri could care less if the family
starved to death. What is an intoxicant in a large amount
is an intoxicant in a small amount. He may have his
vices, but drinking was not one of them.

But the thing which troubled him greatly was the
ongoing drama with his mistress Leila. The women he
slept with all knew the primary rule of play. No
pregnancy. There would be no additional offspring to
challenge his heirs and their right of inheritance under
Islamic law.

Leila Sharif was quite beautiful. She had a Lebanese
father and a French mother. She was the eldest of three
equally stunning sisters. She had soft caramel-colored
eyes set in a porcelain complexion. Her hair was straight,
jet-black and swayed across her buttocks as she walked.
Leila didn't even really walk. She danced across the
room and straight into the heart of every man who ever
laid eyes on her. Khalid Al-Misri had spotted her at a
conference in Beirut where she was serving as a student
representative of Beirut University. He very carefully
cultivated a platonic relationship. She was invited to

major social events in Egypt as a "student representative". The hotel room which awaited her always had a basket of fruit and a large vase of expensive flowers. The first time he bought her a piece of jewelry it was a simple gold bracelet. He took the utmost care not to touch her wrist as he fastened the clasp. When she graduated, he hired her as his personal assistant. His considerable charm, wealth, and worldly maturity took care of the rest. Slam dunk.

Al-Misri was incredibly generous. The look in the eyes of other men when they saw her showed the glimmer of a species in competition for a prize. Every time al-Misri saw "the look" he would open his wallet to his beautiful and loving mistress. Leila's closet overflowed with a rainbow of color. If she mentioned even a small item, perhaps a new necklace, a pair of earrings, she would find it on her pillow within hours. In private circles, al-Misri's chauffeur became known as "Leila's butler".

After sharing an apartment with Leila for a year, al-Misri was so head-over-heels in love that he made a bold financial decision. Seeking out the top real estate broker in Alexandria he located a lovely villa on Kafr Abdu Street near Allenby Park.

Before the Egyptian revolution of 1952 Kafr Abdu Street had also been named after the British High Commissioner and the street connected Rosetta Avenue to the top of the hill where Marshal Allenby had his residence and official headquarters. President Nasser had embarked on an ambitious course of renaming all streets which had British names after he came into office. Fortunately, upscale neighborhoods survive revolutions quite well, and it is usually merely the occupants who change. The villas were snuggled within the lush vegetation and trees which provided a quiet respite from the noisiness of the poorer neighborhoods which surrounded them. Jewel-like and beautiful little cafes provided enjoyable dining experiences. The whole area was a bit surreal, just like the luck he couldn't quite believe – the luck of owning Leila.

It was perfect for a dark beauty whose supple body belonged to the most powerful man in Alexandria. But al-Misri also desperately wanted to possess Leila's very soul. He wanted complete mastery of her emotions, her will, to control the flash in her eyes when she was angry; to bottle the tears that she shed when sad. Her allure was her sense of calm mystery. What was really behind her eyes? What was the message in her laugh?

He felt powerful when he made love to her. But when they were done with the lovemaking? His power lasted but a moment. He became weak in her presence He became even weaker with just the thought of her. So it was that one spring morning Leila found herself with a key pressed into her hand. She opened the door to a home furnished with expensive French antiques, elegant Persian rugs, and each room was filled with vases of fresh cut flowers.

Leila flashed al-Misri with a brilliant smile and simply said, "Come! You must show me our bedroom." As he took her hand, he had the shadow of a thought, "I am no better than the average goat heading to the slaughter."

Things had progressed smoothly for two years after the purchase of the villa. But then the unthinkable happened. Leila became pregnant. She gently announced her pregnancy late one night as they retired to the bedroom. It was in the next breath that she announced her willingness to have an abortion. Searching her lover's face, Leila looked for a sign of distress. Instead, she saw what looked like a deadly snake slither across his face in a slow and deliberate manner. His voice was well-modulated but his countenance had changed.

Secretly, she had hoped that the pregnancy would elicit a marriage proposal. She was willing to be the second wife. It seemed a better status than a pampered mistress. But it was not to be. The news of the need for an abortion was delivered with the same level of emotion with which a man might request a clean towel for his shower.   As a gentleman, al-Misri intended for Leila to have the best of medical care. She was sent to a top professional clinic in London which provided discreet services for the wealthy daughters of Egypt's elite. A pre-abortion sonogram showed that she was only ten weeks along.   That was good. The process of ensoulment had not yet taken place. As far as al-Misri was concerned, Leila was not carrying his child. She was carrying a product of conception. It was not much more than a bug.

After the abortion, Leila recuperated in style and was instructed to take her time shopping for a new wardrobe and whatever delighted her heart.   But when she returned from London, she no longer loved al-Misri. For the first time she felt their relationship was dirty. She considered herself used and cast aside. Initially, the emotional change was not apparent. She continued to sleep with her lover. She gave her body to him fully and complied with whatever suited his mood. But the thoughts in her mind were swimming elsewhere as he poured out his love and lust onto her. She had not been sufficiently sedated for the abortion procedure. She remembered the noise of the suction as the fetus was removed from inside her. In the recovery area she remembered one nurse speaking to another. "She is an astonishingly beautiful woman. Too bad the sperm donor is only interested in her."

The fact that Leila had an abortion changed al-Misri too. Somehow, his passion was now more desperate. His desire for things to return to the normalcy that seemed to exist prior to the pregnancy was intense. But in the last three month the situation had become volatile. It had started with Leila throwing a cup at the wall. It had progressed to her refusal to attend an important dinner with him. Today, al-Misri had reached into his closet to pull out his favorite suit to find that the area where his manhood should be seated had been crudely cut out with a pair of scissors. Leila had stormed out the door to work while he was still in the shower. The ungrateful bitch had become completely crazy. And all of that, over an early term abortion. He just couldn't understand it.

He was so deeply in thought regarding the state of his snipped pants, that at first he did not hear the phone ringing. Startled, he picked it up and heard the voice of Dr. Jamil al-Filisteeni. In a flat voice he heard his friend say, "Khalid's body has been found. I need to leave town for a bit. What do you suggest?"

Al-Misri stood up quickly and a smile spread across his face. Everything came together in his mind clearly now. He thanked god for the way in which things had just come together in his favor. "Jamil, my dear friend! You must come and stay at my villa in Alexandria! I have plenty of room! I will find some consulting work for you and see that you are well-compensated!"

Picking up the phone, he called his office in downtown Alexandria. When Leila answered the phone, his voice dripped with compassion, "Leila, my dear. I have arranged a trip for you to spend a bit of time with your family. I think it will do you good. I have been planning this for a week, but wanted to surprise you. The flight leaves tomorrow morning. It is a first class seat of course. I will give you an ample allowance. As always, it is only the best for my dark-headed beauty!" Hanging up the phone, he said in comical manner, "Only the best for my dark-hearted and ungrateful mistress!" Smiling wickedly, he let out a hoot.

Khalid al-Misri picked up his phone again and called his contact in the foreign ministry. It was simple enough. Leila's visa was to be revoked when she left Egypt. It would be a "procedural mix-up". Al-Misri was assured that a reinstatement of the visa would be delayed for at least a year.   Quite satisfied with himself, Khalid whistled a little tune as he made plans to unload the items in Leila's closet into neatly packed boxes which would follow her home. She was a smart girl. She would figure it out.

The following afternoon, Leila Sharif fell into the arms of her mother with red eyes and a face as pale as death. Overcome with sorrow she wept uncontrollably. Pulling her aside, her mother queried her in staccato manner. "Leila! What can possibly be wrong?" Leila looked at her with the eyes of a frightened young gazelle. " Mother! I took a pharmacy test this morning. I am pregnant and I am so afraid." Her mother began to wail. The sound of her cry was carried all the way to the queue of taxi drivers lined up to carry travelers to their destination. It was a haunting sound which carried fragments of grief into the wind.

Interlude

The Guardian was deep in thought. The wings of the moth were now fluttering dangerously close to the flame. It had been forty-five minutes since he had finished his prayer. But he was still bent over his prayer rug, traveling through the chasms of his mind. Sufism is not words. It is not text. It is a state which is lived in, and anyone who does not taste it, does not know it. Sufism is hal (state), lived in, it is not the word.

The Guardian moved slightly to relieve the cramping sensation which was now kneading his left calf with a steady pain. His mind was now envisioning disturbing images. First he saw a hand moving slowly and in painstaking manner across a sheet of paper. Then he saw a shadow cast over the hand by the bars of a jail cell. This next shard of image was a noose. It was followed with the flight of an emerald green bird. The final image caused beads of sweat to break out on his brow. He saw his staff placed in his hand, his old sandals on his feet and he heard the snort of the steeds of Allah in his ears. Getting up quickly he rubbed his calves vigorously. Moving with a great sense of purpose he awakened the young orphaned houseboy. The child ran the errands in the market each day, in exchange for a place to sleep at night. His manner was quiet and he had learned to be almost as invisible as his benefactor. Asking him to bundle up a few food items and to prepare a leather flask of goat milk, the Guardian then disappeared into the courtyard of the house.

Returning a few minutes later, he accepted the items from the houseboy, who now had quite the look of confusion on his face. The Guardian grabbed his staff and crept silently through the garden gate. Underneath his cloak and securely attached to a belt was a pouch made of camel's hair. The shadows swallowed him up as he fled down the alley. The last thing the little boy heard was the familiar flip-flop of the Guardian's sandals as they made contact with the cobblestones.

Minutes later, the Murid awakened from a deep sleep. Something was wrong. The presence of his Murshid was gone. He saw the small flicker of a kerosene lamp in the kitchen. Seated at the table was the young houseboy. "The master has left." He stated it simply, as if merely announcing the time for afternoon tea. The Murid quickly dressed and also fled through the garden gate. Before leaving he sternly admonished the man child, "Do not leave the house for three days. Do not open the door to anyone." Sadiq nodded his head vigorously.

On the fourth day Sadiq ventured to the corner fruit stand. "Where is your master?" The owner gave him a hard look. Sadiq matched his gaze, "My master has taken ill. He is sleeping in his bed." The owner grunted and reached into his bowl of change which he kept under the table. Handing the boy a coin he said, "Tell your master to come see me. I have had a troubling dream. I saw the steeds of Allah blocking the gate to your master's house." Looking frightened, Sadiq scurried down the street.

Flight

Dr. Khalid al-Misri and Dr. Jamil Nidal al-Filisteeni were seated on the balcony. They watched silently as shadows played across the adjacent villas. The Turkish coffee was strong. Their sentiments were even stronger.

Jamil had just recounted in full measure the events leading up to the disappearance of Marie Claire, and the death of his colleague. He recounted the frantic movements of the courier to Hyderabad, to discover that the Guardian had already fled with the pouch which must be protected by all means and at all times. At this very moment, there was no news concerning the actual escape route and final destination of either the Guardian or his Murhid. Jamil said, "We can assume the student caught up with his master. It is comforting to know the old man has a travel companion. But only Allah knows where they are and until we receive word, there can be no intervention on our end." He then continued his story.

"Undoubtedly, Khalid al-Nur divulged information regarding our national treasure. We are unsure to what

162

extent the information is compromised. But the moment his girlfriend disappeared I knew we were in trouble." Jamil stroked his forehead in worried manner. "I had him followed for two weeks prior to the woman's disappearance." There was just this bad feeling in my gut regarding the relationship. I actually had the physical feeling that I experienced once after consuming an overly-spiced and suspect kebab off the street. Everything looked good on paper. We couldn't find any holes in the woman's story. But Khalid al-Nur was compromised as a good agent. His delivery was sloppy the last time he used our courier. And he was inattentive regarding his professional duties in the office. I brought in a man to do a forensic search of his lap top. The recent history showed searches for wedding rings and family dwellings. He had definitely fallen hard for the little bitch."

"So now we wait," said Khalid al-Misri. "It seems surreal, though." His voice trailed off and then he picked up the thought again. "It is hard to believe that what has been so carefully concealed for so many years might now fall into the hands of the ruthless and hate-mongering Jews. And all this, because your friend couldn't keep his zipper secured."

Jamil hesitated a moment. He began to speak, and then stopped in mid-sentence. His friend looked at him quizzically. "Come on, Jamil. Spit it out. You are holding something back from me. We took the bay'ah together." Jamil saw a pale rage creep up into the face of his counterpart. It started at his lips and went all the way to his forehead. When his face was completely pale, a dark red moon then formed between his eyebrows. But then, he reached out and patted his friend's hand.

Jamil sighed and looked relieved. "I have never been able to keep anything from you." Khalid responded, "Then give me the missing piece to the puzzle. I knew there was something you were leaving out. The matter is entirely too important. Full disclosure belongs to all who have taken the oath of guardianship."

Jamil began to speak again, but this time in a low whisper. "The Murshid fled in the middle of the night only a few minutes after Khalid al-Nur's body was found. According to the police report it was a nosy neighbor who called in the death of Khalid. She called to complain about a suspicious smell coming from the apartment. She claimed it smelled like a meat stew left on the stove. Little did she know! But it is uncanny how the Guardian knew, even before it was made known to me.   We can only hope the scent is cold for the hounds of hell too."

Khalid gave a little snort. "Why should we be surprised?   The Murshid is known for his vivid and accurate dreams. He probably saw the knife as it sliced across the neck." Jamil looked slightly nauseated at the thought.   Unsure of who had been dispatched to bring retribution against Khalid al-Nur, he had a nagging feeling that he might be next.

He had never met the Guardian of the hair of the Prophet, but his reputation for prophetic dreams was quite well-known. He had once foretold the assassination of a world leader. He had seen the whole thing in a dream. Even his move from the Balkans to Hyderabad had been because of a dream. The dream warned of the impending slaughter and the dream guided him to his new location. It was by decree and not by choice, that the Guardian had ended up in Hyderabad. And decree, not choice, would take his feet to his next destination.   Jamil had little doubt regarding his thoughts.. It remained for them to wait with patient endurance. His contact with them would be sudden and surprising.   The message to them would travel tongue-to-tongue. There would be no digital communication for a matter of such importance. The potential compromise of the location of the hair of the Prophet made him shudder involuntarily. But when the message came, one of them, or several of them would have to clear their calendar and move quickly.

That night, as Dr. al-Filisteeni slept, the sights and sounds of his childhood drifted across his consciousness. Most of them, included images of his friend. They were kicking the soccer ball around. There was a vivid image from the funeral of a shaheed. The casket was draped in a Palestinian flag. As the funeral procession moved through the streets the old men held up and jangled the rusted keys hanging from the rings of the homes they had vacated years ago. Allahu Akbar! The sound of their cracked, old voices filled the street. In one image, children were taunting an effigy of an Israeli soldier. The final image was of his deceased friend.

He had been accompanied to the morgue by the police to identify the remains. "Yes," he said, "the silver ring on his right hand is one which I recognize well. This is undoubtedly Khalid al-Nur." Dr. al-Filisteeni asked carefully, "May I remove the ring and send it to his mother?" The staff member handed him a form. "When we are done with the autopsy you may collect the ring."

A week later, when he returned to collect the ring, it had disappeared. "Very strange occurrence," said the clerk. "It is extremely rare that we lose chain of custody of any item."

When Dr. al-Filisteeni awakened the room was still plunged in the darkness of night. Taking his right thumb, he quickly felt for the silver band on his right ring finger. The ring was in identical to the ring which had been worn by Khalid al-Nur. It was a thick silver band with a medium-sized onyx stone. What was known only to those who wore the ring was what was carefully encased within the silver beneath the onyx setting. It was the thin scalish thread of a date fruit. Those tasked with the protection of the hair of the Prophet all wore the same ring. Each one was identical. Each wore a ring as a reminder of the oath they had taken. It had not been an oath taken under a tree, but there had been greater secrecy involved. Things could not be done in open manner.

When Dr. al-Filisteeni sat down to breakfast with al-Misri that morning, his friend surprised him by the first words which came out of his mouth. "Jamil, it is time that we use alpha protocol for any communication of importance regarding the Hair of the Prophet

Muhammad (PBUH). As such, I have drafted a letter to be sent by courier to all members of the Shura Council. We must both put our rings to good use. These letters, require a double wax seal." Dr. Jamil al-Filisteeni ran his thumb across his ring again. "I am in agreement. It is time to move forward with the alpha protocol."

Placing their rings into warm wax the two men carefully sealed each letter. The letters were put into a sandalwood box. Jamil turned to his countepart. "How can you assure the contents of the box will not be intercepted?" Al-Misri laughed, "Who can move with greater ease than a diplomatic courier? There is little need to worry."

Colonel Ari Barak

Colonel Ari Barak hurled curses at the wall of his office. Picking up the telephone he quickly dialed Yuri Cohen. When Yuri picked up the phone, the voice at the other end was thick with blood, "Cohen! Khalid al-Nur has been murdered. Our agent has secured one item of interest from the morgue. It is being sent by courier to our research labs. Otherwise, we have nothing." Yuri gave an emphatic grunt. "Then it is even more important that we put our team in motion immediately. The Sufi are notorious for their impenetrable escape tunnels. They are worse than the average mole. It is possible the target has completely skipped the continent."

Col. Ari Barak picked up the phone again and dialed Vice Admiral Seigel. "Joshua, this is Ari. Has our operative arrived yet?" The Vice Admiral glanced toward the tarmac. "She has just disembarked from her flight." Col. Barak spoke in a voice which his friend recognized as the tone he reserved for when he was royally pissed off. "Assemble your best memory retrieval team and top psychiatrist. Throw in your best hypnotist. When you are done with my useless intelligence operative, march her back to me."

In a dry tone which masked his sudden interest Vice Admiral Seigel responded, "What do you have planned?" Col. Barak gave a short and wicked laugh, "I intend to locate a three hundred pound bureaucrat with vile manners with zero intelligence value. My operative will wash herself out of the program after her next assignment." As he hung up the phone, Vice Admiral Seigel smiled in spite of himself.   Glancing out the window he noted the woman was quite good-looking. He felt a twinge of regret for what awaited her. Two days later, Marie Claire found herself seated across from Col. Ari Barak again. He looked rested. She felt like she had aged ten years.

At one point during the memory retrieval exercise she had signed a medical consent for small titrated doses of intravenous benzodiazepines to assist the hypnotist with his task. For some reason, the whole process had left her feeling violated. She had suffered an intellectual rape. And the predators were members of her own intelligence community. It was one thing to do it to someone else. It was a completely different experience when on the receiving end of the tender mercies of the information extraction team.

Col. Barak looked at her with his wolfish eyes and flashed a smile. "You have done excellent work. We would like to send you to Sharm el-Sheikh for a week. Enjoy the warm breezes. Even take your mother along, if you wish. Then you will be sent along to your next assignment. You need to be far away from the urban landscape We have assigned you to an absolutely exotic locale."

Sliding a file across the table, Marie Claire felt she was taking a piece of meat from a rabid dog. Opening it, she glanced at the image of her next target. His eyes were recessed down into rolls of facial fat. His chin draped over the knot in his tie. He looked like he had slept in his suit. The name was one she couldn't pronounce. The country code was one she did not recognize. Keeping her voice calm she said, "Col. Ari, if you please. I am unfamiliar with this particular country code. Looking at her with a squared smile, he replied, "The code denotes Bhutan. It is a lovely place. I have been there myself. It is a land which time has forgotten." His script was one which did not evade her. It was a land time had forgotten. Her punishment was to be of the kind which not only denied her intellect but also trampled on her femininity.

Now flashing a formidable and brilliant smile, he stood up and gestured to the door. Marie Claire thought he had the look of a gladiator. It was the professional posture she had admired in the past. Now she only felt an unsettling sense of fear. Too much had transpired in too rapid a manner. That was the way the intelligence machine worked, in nanoseconds, if need be. But Marie Claire was not a machine. She was exhausted to the core of her being. The information extraction team had peeled her like an onion, in the same casual manner a chef would peel an onion. But they were master chefs. And when they told her things about her personality, her deep psyche, that she barely understood herself, it caused a deep sense of danger. Marie Claire stood slowly. The bones in her legs felt as if they had turned to liquid. Her face felt strangely numb. Moving slowly, she crossed over into the corridor. It had seemed quite bright in times past. Now, the corridor looked like a dark tunnel.

Tipping Point

Two files, identical copies, were side-by-side on the conference table. Two sets of hands opened the files silently.

Case file 11097-267

Agent Code: P574
Gender: female

Activity: Memory Retrieval Exercise

Officer in Charge: Dr. Jonathan Weiss

Title: Chief of Psychiatric Services

After two days of intense testing the results are as follows:

- Administration of all phases of memory retrieval methodologies were employed with Agent P574. An algorithm which uses passive and peaceful means of memory retrieval was used for the first eight hours of interaction. This was followed by an algorithm which introduced aggressive psychological stressors into the environment.
- Data input and subsequent analysis provided a negligible intelligence field.
- Profile analysis concurrently run with the memory retrieval attempt show a highly confident operative willing to take risks. Yet the test results from the profile reveal an agent who is marginally adept at intuitive guesswork. She lacks the powerful substratum known as intuitive intelligence gathering. The capability to plunder intelligence from subliminal thought patterns is lacking. We introduced phrases from conversations with her target during the passive phase of memory retrieval. Results depict an agent with adequate analytical grasp, yet lacking the paranormal bridge mechanism which is the hallmark of the top two percent of our highest yield field officers.

- Agent P574 appeared to deploy a blocking mechanism, or perhaps a protective barrier, regarding certain aspects of her targets activities and acquaintances. Mild Stockholm syndrome is apparent, albeit, this is noted with female agents on the third or fourth assignment. It is rarely seen within male agents for reasons of gender-specific biochemistry.

Recommendations in order of precedence:

*Return to the field within a protected habitat affording a lower level of play.

*Process for discharge.

Dr. Jonathan Weiss
Chief of Psychiatric Services

Colonel Ari Barak and Yuri Cohen closed the files. Yuri Cohen walked to the window which overlooked a small courtyard. "What do you want me to do regarding this agent, Colonel Barak?" There was a long silence. "Perhaps I was a bit hard on her. But on the other hand, if the agent is incapable of capturing an extremely important intelligence signal it does not bode well for her career."

"Should I process her for administrative separation?"

Col. Barak bent over to tighten his bootlace. When he looked up his eyes had changed. It was the look of a wolf in his secure lair. "Extend her vacation a week. Process her for administrative separation. Give her the standard severance package. But make sure that I never see her again within this compound. Her clearance level is to be officially scrubbed." With that, Col. Barak turned on his heel and left the room.

Yuri Cohen was stunned. He felt a small hard pit forming in his stomach. He had passed Marie Claire in the hallway as she left Col. Barak's office. Her face was ashen. But she had managed to smile at him. That showed discipline and emotional strength. He had always admired her from afar. She managed to separate out the aspects of her double life better than many of the agents he had worked with in the past.

Sure, what he would do was by direction. It was straight from the books and just like it should be within a chain of command. But the task was distasteful. The women gave so much more of themselves than the men. He knew it. He had married a former field agent. They had three lovely children. But there were the rare nights when she talked in her sleep. Some things, a country should never ask, of the women. Some things, a man should never hear, from the lips of his wife.

Opaque

A child could have pulled off surveillance on this particular day. Yuri felt a strange compassion for his professional colleague. He watched as Marie Claire moved aimlessly through the streets. Her gait seemed stilted. She had the look of someone who has eyes wide open, but the images being imprinted on the brain are not ones of the present, but ones from the past. To be sure, he brushed past her. She did not give a sign of recognition. Circling back around, he continued to follow her. Not once, did she use her telephone. No word came from her lips to those who passed by her, the men who would greet her with a smile. Even under duress, Marie Claire was a great beauty. It was almost as if Yuri had a front row seat to some macabre dance of the dead. He had little doubt that Marie Claire felt dead inside.

Finally, he had enough. Moving slowly toward her, and matching her stride, he spoke her name. She ignored him. "Marie Claire. Let me acquire a vehicle. I will take you wherever you wish to go. But you must not stay on the streets."

Yuri stalked out of the hotel lobby after paying for a

room for Marie Claire at one of the finer establishments in the city. He arranged for a massage therapist to come to her room later that evening. He ordered a bottle of wine, a plate of fruit with hand-dipped chocolates. It was all that he could do, prior to delivering the cruel blow the following day. He strode to his car. Seeing the vehicle of one of his counterparts, a man who was having an affair in rather open manner with one of the lower-level analysts, fed his anger. He viciously keyed the car door. Slipping into his own vehicle he gunned the engine and headed for his favorite bar. He couldn't even think of issuing the order for administrative separation unless minimally drunk. Gripping the steering wheel tightly, he rolled down the window to allow the wind to slap him in the face. Yuri picked up his phone and placed a call to his wife. "Can you meet me for a drink?"

Yuri and Deborah were seated in one of the tiny alcoves of the bar reserved for special clientele. That clientele included both senior executives and top government officials. The proprietor was a man with a keen sense of the need for privacy amongst those engaged in serious business transactions. He had become wealthy because of his ability to combine skill and discretion within his profession. More than a few of his lucrative financial investments had been accomplished outside the bounds of what is taught the average student at the better business establishments. When he had gutted and redesigned the interior of the facility it had been with a remarkable eye for detail. He created the five compact alcoves with people like Yuri Cohen in mind. There was ample distance from the main floor space of the bar. One server was assigned to the patrons within the alcoves. A buzzer beneath each table allowed them to alert staff of the need for refreshed drinks or a food order. The server moved within the alcoves like a ghost. It was a position which was highly guarded by the three men who rotated within this exclusive and highly valued space. The work was easy and the gratuities were spectacular.

Yuri had just ordered a second bottle of wine and was telling his wife the skeletal details of the case. Deborah looked at her husband with sympathetic eyes. "We cannot afford mistakes on this scale. The Americans have run slipshod operations since the time of their peace-loving President Carter. HumInt was degraded. The fascination with technology created a class of pompous tattlers who did little more than repeat the digital news of the day. Your operative did not know the nature of her find. But I fault her for lack of initiative and not taking the leap into the paranormal to run with her gut. You know that a paranormal leap of my own once brought a critical piece of intelligence to the eyes of our superiors."

Deborah looked at her husband quizzically and ran her finger across the top of her wine glass. "Tell me the true nature of what is in the pouch. We don't spend millions of dollars to recover fourteen grey hairs." Yuri looked at his wife with the professional respect which he had always felt for her. Reaching to grasp her hand, he gently squeezed her fingers. "You know I cannot give full disclosure. As it is, the Americans are in the dark regarding this issue. And only a handful of officers know the true content of the pouch. But we do consider it a critical security mission."

Deborah gently removed her hand from that of her husband. She suddenly ached to return to the field. She had never felt more alive than when in pursuit of the enemies of Israel. "What of the operatives tasked with securing the pouch?" Yuri leaned closer to his wife and whispered in her ear, "They are seasoned field agents. They are also cognizant this is the highest priority mission to be engaged on behalf of Israel in the past decade."

"Then swallow your guilt, Yuri. We cannot afford to keep agents like the one in question in the field. She has shown herself to be a liability to the service. Send her home. She will find a decent man and put her ovaries to good use."

Yuri smiled at his wife. "Isn't that exactly what you did?" Deborah returned the smile, "Sure. But I left the service because I wanted to sleep with a man I loved, not with men I despised.

Yuri smiled fondly at his wife. She always set his mind at ease regarding his administratively distasteful duties. He was just glad that Colonel Ari Barak had not set his eyes on her first. She was clever, but kind.

Redux

Chief Inspector Banks sat at his desk and ran his fingers across the mahogany. It had taken him thirty-five miserable years to attain his current rank as Chief Inspector of Campione and the greater Lake Lugano district. He had been shoved against the wall, crapped on and kicked around many times during his climb to the top. But he was aware that he had done the same to his professional peers. No hard feelings. He had always been part of bare knuckles police force. After the early years of driving a patrol car he had managed to make selection for the undercover narcotics squad. His plan was simple enough. He set up a couple of lower level drug dealers for busts and then muscled his way into information leading to the arrest of a regional drug distributor. Confiscating some of the contraband, he preyed upon a few more unfortunate souls who suddenly and unwittingly found themselves in possession of drugs and paraphernalia which they had never laid eyes on before. He was no better than the fireman who sets buildings ablaze to watch the glory of the flames and then "find" the evidence.

Banks established himself as a sort of folk hero, the officer on the beat with the uncanny ability to sniff out the drug dealers on the street. When he was eventually selected for the narcotics squad he diligently learned every trick which was passed his way.

From the narcotics squad, he moved into the ranks of the homicide division. Initially, he was assigned to the easy cases.   But after taking a couple of university courses in forensic science, he proved adept at solving the cold case murders in his district. He groomed himself for greater things.   His flair for dealing with the media always put him in good stead with his superiors. His dedication to the job eventually cost him two marriages and the alienation of his only daughter. He was rarely at home. And when he was home he brought the work with him. Driven to succeed, he had finally reached his goal. For some reason, the feeling which he expected to wash over him never occurred.

Reaching for a cold case file he began to review the sketchy investigation of an event which had happened in 1963, the death of a housekeeper at an estate a few miles from his headquarters. He then opened a much thicker folder. It was the folder which he had kept at home, ever since he received the reprimand for exposing the dereliction of duty of his superior. The time felt right, to voice his concern again. Picking up the telephone, he placed a call to Interpol.

Two weeks later a comprehensive raid was carried out at the estate in Campione. What was found sent a jolt through the intelligence community. But for Chief Inspector Banks, it was merely a moment of vindication for the time his ass had been handed to him on a platter so many years ago. He watched as crates of documents were loaded into awaiting vans. The vehicles disappeared into the early morning mist. His contact from Interpol clapped his hand across his shoulder twice and commented casually, "Maybe this will all turn out to be nothing. But just to tie up any loose ends, I will send someone along to collect your personal files." Smiling broadly, he jumped into an awaiting vehicle. Turning to the driver he said, "The damn son of a bitch doesn't have a clue, does he? Send along an official letter thanking him for his diligence. Don't put any words in the letter with more than two syllables. He will have a rough time reading it."

Booty

Colonel Ari Barak had personally selected the track and trap teams in Washington, D.C. and Hyderabad. The team in the United States was tasked with entering the labyrinth and locating Ariadne's thread. But it was the team in Hyderabad which would fully enter the game to locate the hair of the Prophet Muhammad. The second team had the toughest of assignments. A camel through the eye of a needle seemed an easier task.

Col. Barak was always an optimist based on his own experience in HumInt. He had taken to heart the words of his operational trainer on the day he was handed his initial field assignment.

Leopold Weinstein was a Hungarian Jew. His family had weathered the ravages and deep injustices which swept across Europe during the Nazi reign of terror. Although a young child at the time, he distinctly remembered two things: bitter cold and biting hunger. These things can kill or make the man. In the case of Weinstein, the trauma of childhood was turned to unflinching resolve during his adulthood. He gave his energies and spent his adulthood working for the state of

Israel. Any entity or individual designated as an enemy of the state became his own personal enemy. The agency considered him a dedicated asset with ruthless instincts. His love for Israel surpassed any other concern. Or so was the imagination of his counterparts in the intelligence sector.   The real reason for his resolve was for the protection of his own progeny. Each day in which he kept them safely quartered and provisioned was a day in which he reveled in his masculine identity.

On the day he sat across the table to discuss Col. Barak's first field operation the look on his face was grim. As he gripped the folder in his hand, his knuckles had the whiteness of the pale horse rider of an apocalyptical tale.

"An Israeli mother and her pregnant daughter were abducted, raped and killed by a gang of thugs five days ago. They were shopping in Beirut. Their chauffeur was seated in their vehicle a block away when the incident transpired. They were targeted by unknown assailants but the calculated guess is it was members of HizbAllah. The abduction happened so quickly. It took only a few seconds and would have taken less time, had the one woman not been unwieldy due to the Jewish child in her womb. Available witnesses have offered only vague details regarding the vehicle and features of the assailants. But we do know the women were targeted. When their naked and mutilated bodies were recovered the mother had a piece of paper in her mouth. It said, 'Death to all Jews'. The autopsy results show that both women were raped via all available orifices. Nothing was left to the imagination. The autopsy on the fetus leads us to believe the intrauterine death was possibly an hour prior to the maternal death. The fetus died from the externally inflicted beating to the mother and the violence of the rape. In her case, it appears that instrumentation was involved in the rape of the vaginal vault. The medical examiner recovered a splinter of wood from the vaginal cuff. The pregnant female put up quite the fight. Her mother merely showed a few defensive wounds with skin tissue recovered from under her fingernails. She was a bit older and knew they did not stand a chance. I want this to sink into your psyche, Ari. Three generations of Jews died at the hands of merciless hatred. This is not the Holocaust. But it is a tragedy for the families."

Ari Barak opened the file. It took him less than two minutes to read the entire report. But he read it again and allowed the names of the victims to burn their way into his psyche. When he lifted his eyes to look at Leopold he noted a mixture of amusement and what appeared to be a flicker of anger.

"The information available means you will have to function as a man tracking an apparition. But I do not doubt that you will be successful. This is exactly why I have chosen you for the honor of leading this team into the kill box. We are much better than our American counterparts. They have become lazy and dependent on their tech toys for intelligence. We continue to operate with firm belief that eyes and feet on the ground will far surpass any technological front if we continue to train our operatives properly. The Americans will pay for their folly in the future. We predict, even now, their nation will suffer an attack of such magnificent proportions they will find the scope of the operation against them unbelievable. They have forgotten how to navigate the subterranean passages of human intelligence. They have also grown soft. They shed a tear and show too much angst when an operative is lost. That is not our manner of doing business with our enemies. It is blood for blood and not teardrop for teardrop. We leave the tears to the women. Our eyes remain dry or we lose focus. We can ill-afford any deconstruction of our human intelligence due to our distinct geographic limitations. And we will be damned if we deconstruct our human intelligence missions to function little better than having station chiefs seated within our embassies with their cadres of operatives locating 'intelligence' in the regional newsprint. Do I make it abundantly clear how we expect this operation to end? I am placing unlimited financial resources at your disposal."

Ari tapped his fingers on the table and then he ran his fingers through his hair a bit nervously. "Which team members are available to me and what is an expected timeline for mission completion?" Weinstein shot back, "Whatever you require and as long as it takes. We will pull any man off his existing mission if you consider him critical to mission completion. We will loan him to you for as long as there is a need."

Three months later Ari returned to Tel Aviv. Four men responsible for the deaths of the Israeli women were dead. Two of the men had a firstborn son. They were also dead. The Angel of Death did his work quickly and in efficient manner. The rider on the pale horse is also an apparition. The code name for the operation had been aptly chosen: Pale Horse.

A week later Ari was seated in a debriefing room with the husband of the pregnant woman.

The husband of the deceased had powerful connections within the government. He had readily signed the secrecy act paperwork and now looked in expectant manner at the officer seated across from him. Ari looked at the man and said, "What you are allowed to see in this room is to stay in this room. You must never speak of it with anyone. Should you do so, we will know. Appropriate action will be taken. The action, will be beyond the arm of legal defense for you." The man nodded solemnly. Ari opened a folder and pulled out four black and white photos. "These are the men who killed your wife and firstborn son." Opening a second folder he said, "These are the firstborn sons of the men who killed your firstborn son." Ari paused for a moment. He assessed the man carefully and continued. "We will not release the autopsy report for your wife and firstborn offspring. But let me note that the fate of these men and their sons was merciful and quite unlike the manner in which your family suffered unimaginable brutality."

After the man viewed the images again he rose slowly to his feet and extended his hand to Ari. Giving a firm handshake he thanked him for executing justice on behalf of his bloodline. Clasping his shoulder firmly Ari responded, "This lesson will not soon be forgotten by the enemies of Israel." After the man left, Ari lit a cigarette. Picking up the folders he looked at the images again. The deaths had been accomplished in efficient manner. For some odd reason, he felt a sensation of pleasure surge over him. He felt a strong prickling sensation at the back of his neck. Satisfied with his work, he bounded the stairs to return the files to the archives.

As Col. Ari now stood looking out his window this particular day he also recognized the feeling of pleasure which washed across him. There were men who liked to chase skirts. He liked to chase the enemies of Israel across the globe. Picking up the phone, he called the team heading to Hyderabad. They would arrive within the next hour. He wanted to reiterate the importance of the mission. On a deeper level, it was the action of the lead wolf in the pack communicating with his bare-fanged brethren. In unconscious manner he ran his fingers through his hair.

Reconnaissance

Once in Hyderabad, the Israeli team would require the highest level of tracking skills ever used by the agency. The pouch was secured by a secretive Sufi organization. Sufism presented as a Gordian knot with regard to successful tracking. The Masters were not easily traced through standard methods. They seemed to have a freakish paranormal means of travel and they could disappear from the landscape for months at a time. When they reappeared from their damn worm holes, there was no telling where they had been. Nor was there any clue regarding what they had done during their unaccounted for absences.

Their presence was noted by the global intelligence community. But any absence could be a cause for concern. They were sentinels of events looming on the horizon. It was amazing how one of these guys could disappear into thin air. A region vacated by a Sufi master would explode into conflict or be hit with a cataclysmic disaster a week after his disappearance. There would be the assassination of a leader, a major revolt, or the forces of nature would come together to release thousands of human souls from their bodies. The Sufi masters were like the twenty or so Grand Ayatollah currently living across the globe. They didn't die of disease. They died of damned old age. Too bad Israeli intelligence couldn't harness their powers.

The men remained hard as hell to track if they took flight. Colonel Barak remembered the time he had attended an intelligence gathering summit in London dedicated to the topic of Sufism. The final speaker had ended his PowerPoint presentation with a picture of a flying red carpet with flock of birds flying alongside it. His final words were glum. "Perhaps they still have the flying carpet used by Suleiman and his army of avian couriers." The group had laughed uproariously. But at the moment, Col. Barak was throwing invectives against the wall. Intermingled with his cursing was the name of a woman he now hated with an intensity which he hadn't felt for years. Marie Claire.

Colonel Barak opened his desk and pulled out a bottle and measured two fingers of brandy into a shot glass. He rarely drank prior to the end of a long work day but today was different. His nerves felt a bit frayed. Glancing at himself in the mirror of the bathroom moments earlier his hairline seemed to have a bit more gray than the prior week. He had slept very little in the previous forty-eight hours and the calls from his wife had gone unheeded. She knew the drill. When he did not respond, the matter was of national importance.

Taking a sip from his glass he reflected back on his career. His mind took him back to the beginning point of intelligence training. In his mind's eye he saw the professor who taught analytical intelligence. The first reading assignment had been "Das Glasperlenspeil" by Hermann Hesse. Fair enough. The students were fluent in German and the majority had read the novel in college. The test which followed was quite a different story. Opening their laptops and keying in their randomly assigned passwords for the day the students were greeted with a screen with Arabic script. The complete test was in Arabic and their answers and accompanying handwritten essays were also to be in Arabic. Col. Barak remembered with unusual clarity the day he received his test result. He was given a failing grade because he had omitted one diacritical mark near the end of his essay. His professor was merciless. Fixing him with a stern gaze he said, "We do not have years to teach you to play the game well. Israel is under daily attack even as you are seated comfortably on this campus as a guest of the intelligence community. We need for you to rise to the top quickly to grasp abstract synthesis and also to develop the paranormal skills which make deep strategic connections between seemingly unrelated events. Leaving the diacritical mark off the word shows a sloppy work ethic."

Ari noticed the slight but intentional decibel change in the voice of his professor when he said the word "guest". He was also aware the session was being recorded. Deliberately relaxing the tension in his fingers he looked directly into the eyes of his professor. "It will never happen again. I give you my oath that I will diligently seek to never make the same mistake twice."

His mind then moved to the first and only time when he had killed a woman in the line of duty. He remembered how it felt to slip the ligature around her neck as she stood in the shower. She should have never approached him in the bar. She made the fatal mistake of inviting him up to her room. Fair is fair. He was the better agent. She would have killed him if he hadn't gotten to her first. There could be no mercy when it came to the protection of Israel and the government's secrets.

His mind floated to that day long ago when he had killed an elderly Russian gentleman seated on a pier. It occurred to him that there was not any emotion of guilt attached to the killing of a woman or an elderly and defenseless man. He only felt satisfaction. Lifting his glass to his lips he drank again. Of course he should feel satisfaction. The game required a special breed of intelligent bastards. Col. Barak considered himself one of the best.

Pulling himself out of his reverie he picked up the phone and dialed his home. When his wife answered he simply said, "I will be home tonight. Let me take you and the children out for dinner."

The Shura Council

Dr. Bilal Stephens had just finished a vigorous game of basketball with a group of junior high boys who attended his masjid. Patting each one of them on the shoulder, he reminded them to attend the evening prayers. Dr. Stephens had an iron-clad rule. When the men who attended daily prayers had a son arriving at the tenth year of life he would request a meeting with the father and his son. The meeting was always in his office. It was best to exert his authority effectively with a territorial backdrop. Sure, the whole earth was a masjid. A man could pray anywhere. And the dust of the earth could be used for ablution. But the masjid was Muslim land. It was land which belonged to the Muslims and the jurisdiction of Allah. So beyond arranging a meeting, the staff was advised there were to be no interruptions.

The meeting would begin with a discussion from a work by Sayyid Qutb. Dr. Stephens would open his Arabic copy of "Milestones" and read the text. He would then reach for an English transliteration and read the same aloud:

When the number of Believers reaches three, then this faith tells them; "Now you are a community, a distinct Islamic community, distinct from that jahili society which does not live according to this belief or accept its basic premise.   Now the Islamic society has come into existence."

Closing the English copy of text, Dr. Stephens would then look straight into the eyes of the young man. He would now quote again, and in Arabic, the words he had just read in English.

Looking with both intent and kindness at the young boy, who was by now looking a bit terrified, Dr. Stephens would throw out the challenge. "Your father and I alone do not make a distinct Islamic community. Are you ready to join us and to do your part?"

So it was that on an afternoon in his office with a father and a son, the secretary knocked quietly on the door and asked permission to enter. Dr. Stephens was a bit startled when he heard her soft voice say, "It is of the greatest urgency. A courier has delivered a letter addressed to you. The envelope advises that you open it immediately." His secretary seemed to glide into the room and the interruption to his tradition lasted only a few seconds. He noted the double wax seal and completely lost his train of thought. Excusing himself briefly, he left his office and seated himself in the library. What he read brought a sense of anxiety to his heart.

"It is imperative the Shura Council meet as quickly as possible. The Guardian is dead. The pouch is secure for the moment. The murid is in possession of his own ring. But we must determine a course of action."

With trembling fingers Dr. Stephens carefully refolded the message and slid it between the pages of a favorite commentary. The Hair of the Prophet Muhammad was safe. The faces which had just moments before been seated in front of him now seemed like a blur of obscurity and anonymity. His memory took him back to a meeting in Switzerland, the later meeting in London, the trip to the Sufi shrine in Hyderabad. A few moments later he became aware that his guests were looking at him quizzically. He returned to the present and continued the instruction. Looking across the desk at the young man who now awaited his further guidance he smiled gently. Speaking in a moderated tone he continued as if there had been no interruption.

Al-Zalzala

The Architect moved slowly about his home. He was deep in thought. Earlier in the day he had received a call from a close personal friend in Istanbul. Turkiye Buyuk Millet Meclisi was in the midst of a political upheaval. The tumult could be to his advantage in the future. He wanted desperately to return to Istanbul. The city had such a cosmopolitan flair. Thus far, all attempts at return had been blocked by the government. But the call had left him with moist eyes. It had been years since he had shed a tear. But the occasion seemed to call for it. When he hung up, he cried in the manner in which only the displaced of the earth can understand. America was not his home. Not in the most real sense of the word. The sights and sounds were different. The water was not the same. The seasonal fragrance which whirled through the trees was distinct from the smell from the trees surrounding the village of his birth. Most certainly, nothing comparable could be found for the sensory stimulation provided by Istanbul.

He had also received the delivery of a letter which had shaken him to the very core. The hair of the Prophet Muhammad was safe. The members of the Shura Council would convene as quickly as possible for consultation. One of them would be selected to bring the pouch safely to the United States. It was imperative the Shura Council have full access to the contents prior to determining who would be selected to assume the chain of custody for the irreplaceable treasure. A new Guardian would be selected. All would occur in due time. But this moment, brought a deep level of sentiment which was like an earthquake deep within his psyche.

The Architect knew that he could not travel abroad to retrieve the pouch. But he was filled with tremendous longing when imagining his reaction. His eyes would see that which he had longed to see from the first time he had been made aware of its existence.

The Architect was a Hafiz. Not an ordinary Hafiz. He was also one of the most foremost scholars of the life and works of both Hasan al-Banna and Sayyid Qutb. He comforted himself with the Qur'an and the Sunnah of the Prophet. But he invigorated his intellect with memorized writings of Sayyid Qutb. The works might be banned in Egypt. But no man could ban what was within the cobbled paths of his mind.

Stepping onto the deck at the back of his home, the Architect began to quote from "Milestones". His voice rang out with the cadence of a Believer.

"The callers to Islam in every country and in every period should give thought to one particular aspect of the history of Islam, and they should ponder over it deeply. This is related to the method of inviting people to Islam and its way of training.

At one time this Message created a generation – the generation of the Companions of the Prophet, may God be pleased with them – without comparison in the history of Islam, even in the entire history of man. After this, no other generation of this caliber was ever again to be found. It is true that we do find some individuals of this caliber here and there in history, but never again did a great number of such people exist in one region as was the case during the first period of Islam. This is an obvious and open truth of history, and we ought to ponder over it deeply so that we may reach its secret....."

Looking down at his ring finger he lightly touched the onyx stone. He quoted An Nisa 77. Then he took his letter and read it one more time. Entering his office he lit the large candle on his desk. As the pages of the letter curled and danced in the flame he felt himself close to his Lord.

The wings of the moth fluttered closer and closer to the flame. The Architect felt beads of sweat on his forehead. Groaning loudly, he felt the surge of power rushing through his veins. Annihilation.

The Best of all Planners

Colonel Ari Barak looked glumly out the window of his office. Perhaps it was time to consider resigning his post. It was all about timing when considering when to pass the shield to the next generation of warriors.

The prior month had been hard on him. His career and frequent absences were hard on his children. And in the last week he had been pulled aside by a colleague and notified that his wife was having an affair. He remembered the words of the officer from Internal Security as he delivered the bad news straight to his face. It was accompanied by a folder containing images of his wife with her lover. "The state of Israel does not give a damn about the sex life of the citizens. It does give a damn about the extra-marital affairs of the spouse of a senior intelligence officer. Your wife's affair could compromise national security." Col. Barak looked his counterpart straight in the eye and said, "Thank you for making me aware of this situation. Obviously, I am the last to know about it."

Things had not gone well when he gently confronted his wife with her indiscretion. Deep down inside he knew that he deserved the episode of infidelity. He couldn't blame her for alleviating her loneliness in the usual manner. He had been a good provider but never a good husband. There were weeks when his work pushed him to the point of exhaustion. He had little left to give to the children on his arrival home. He responded in rote manner as he checked their homework or answered their questions about his day. He had even less to give to his wife when overseeing field operatives actively pursuing a critical and time-sensitive mission.

The latest field operation had ended in a fiasco. The state of Israel had a dead Sufi saint on their hands. The Sufi master had been located at a small masjid on the outskirts of Beirut. He had been kidnapped from a nearby street corner shortly after the evening prayers. But it quickly became apparent that he had purposefully made his appearance to function as a decoy. The pouch with the hair of the Prophet was not on his person. All that he possessed of interest was a silver ring with an onyx stone inscribed with the name of Allah in Arabic. The ring had been sent to the metallurgical lab for analysis.

The murid has, of course, conveniently disappeared from the face of the earth. The pouch is still out in the wind and the trail as cold as a goat path through the

Himalayas.   Obviously, his master has taught him the tricks of the trade. "Damn the paranormal bastards", he thought.   The pouch had disappeared into thin air.

In what was the biggest feat of paranormal power, the Sufi had proclaimed to his captors that he would die shortly before the Fajr prayer. The old man was found dead the following morning before dawn broke across the horizon. He was found slumped on the floor beside his cot. His body was still warm and his eyes were still open, as if seeing what is unseen.

When Col. Barak read the report of the untimely death, he felt the hair stand up on the back of his neck. Damn the Sufi. They had a bag of tricks at their disposal. And the best of all tricks is to die before an effective interrogation can secure actionable intelligence.

Reaching into a desk drawer Col. Barak pulled out a cigarette and put it to his lips. He made a mental note that he had smoked nearly two packs today. His usual routine was less than a pack a day. Walking to the couch at the far end of his office he suddenly felt extreme fatigue. Perhaps it was the multiple nights with a sleep pattern which barely counted as a long afternoon nap. Perhaps it was the pounding headache which had started at the base of his skull and now traveled to his scalp.

Crushing the cigarette in a tray he called his secretary. "Hold all calls for me for the remainder of afternoon." Slumping down into the couch he fell into a restless sleep. When Col. Barak awakened his office was bathed in darkness. Flipping onto his other side, he returned to the troubled thoughts swirling into his dreams.

In one dream, Col. Barak was speaking to the 2001 graduates from the asymmetrical warfare class which was held within the basement spaces of the building. As he spoke, his voice boomed out over the podium. "The concept of a world dominant government of Allah is something which has been swaddled through the centuries in neonate state.   Islam has awaited with patient endurance this 21st century. The confines of a strong political ideology nourished in secret observance for centuries, and carried along by the Sufi, has been stripped of its bindings. We are aware of the difficulties which await us. Our American counterparts remain clueless. The Americans and the British have walked into a historical timeline which will shake to the core their diplomats, top strategy analysts, and leaders of government. Their idealism of the past, the trust they have placed in their ability to manipulate the geopolitical chessboard, will soon be a thing of remote memory. They are mismatched both ideologically and politically at this point in time. All necessary components are in place geographically, politically and technologically for Islam to sweep the globe. We intercepted a Hadith communication recently with a cryptic message attached. 'Islam must soon dominate the world'. Top flight Islamic scholars are in agreement regarding the Hadith which states that in the last days the sun will rise in the West. That 'sun' is Islam. There will be a renaissance of Islam in the West. America in particular, is seen as the most desirable of targets. The European organizational counterparts are burdened with a larger class of functionally illiterate and undereducated Muslim immigrants. The Muslim bread basket in Europe will contain bigger pieces of moldy bread. America is the destination of choice for the top scholars. And America is the prize. A healthy democracy is the best place to install a vibrant geopolitical Islam. And the tools of democracy will achieve theocracy. Whether functioning on the lowest levels with cultural memory or moving to highest levels of consolidated thought regarding a global plan, the premiere political organization of a 21st century Islam will continue to work based on decade incremental script.

Apart from the script are the decade incremental operational considerations."

As Col. Barak began to move slowly to awareness of his surroundings, he willed himself back into the sleep cycle. When his speech continued he saw himself still behind the podium. But the faces of the students had changed. They were now the faces of the men and women who resided under his chain of command. It was the men and women tasked with securing a Sufi and his valuable pouch.

"The information collected and analyzed from the safe house in Switzerland was quite valuable. Unfortunately, we have failed to secure the pouch containing the hair of the Prophet. Without that piece of the puzzle, we remain as blind men groping in the darkness."

Col. Barak sat bolt upright with the sound of incessant ringing from the telephone coming from his desk. Dawn had yet to unfurl her pink fingers across the sky. Glancing at his watch he realized that he had slept for eleven hours.

Labyrinth

Dr. Dawud Malik had just finished breakfast when his wife handed him the phone. The voice on the other end was one he knew well. "Shaheed! What brings you creeping into my house with a phone call at such an early hour?" There was a long pause and Dr. Malik heard the sound of a voice caught in the throat, a surreal sound edged with a tinge of shock. "Dr. Malik, my respected father passed away early this morning. Innalilall ah-e-Wa inna ilaih-e-Rajiaoon." Now it was Dr. Malik's turn to be shocked. "What were the circumstances of his death?" Shaheed responded, "My mother found him on his prayer rug. He was cold. His eyes were fixed. There was no pulse." Dr. Malik was silent for a long time, such a long time, that Shaheed blurted out, "Are you still there?" Dr. Malik slowly let out his breath. "I am still here. I am also aware of the list your father gave you asking that certain of us be notified of his passage. I will notify the others."

Shaheed hung up the phone and turned to his mother. Cradling her gently in his arms he noted how frail she seemed. "Dr. Malik will notify the others. I imagine not all of them will be able to come for the funeral prayer." Khadija looked up at her son with a strange look in her eyes. "My son, they are all here. They spent several hours last night with your father in his office." Pausing to let the information sink in she lowered her voice and leaned toward her son's ear, even though they were the only two living souls in the house. "When I entered your father's office to serve the tea I overheard a small snippet of conversation. It seems that a friend of your father also died on his prayer rug right at the time of the Fajr prayer. I am frightened. What does this mean?" Shaheed felt his heart racing a bit and his palms felt quite damp. The week before he had dreamed of his father's death but had told no one and had not sought out the meaning. In his dream, he saw his father and another man, unknown to him, lying dead side by side. The call to prayer was coming from a mosque in Cairo. The dream had troubled him. But now, he was absolutely terrified. "Mother, it means nothing. Allah does as Allah wills."

Khadija ran her fingers across her tear-streaked face and straightened her hijab. "We must make sure your father is treated respectfully. His body must be nicely washed with soap and water. We need the fragrance of camphor. Please obtain the necessary amount to properly prepare your father's body. We have his shroud. I have the three unsewn layers ready and they are perfectly white. Please notify our community members."

Shaheed nodded and said, "This is fard kifaya. My father was a man of standing in the community. Everything will be done according to the Sunnah of Prophet Muhammad (PBUH)." His mother turned and grabbed his hand. "Help me to lift him and place him on the bed." With that, she fled toward her husband and collapsed onto the floor beside him. The sound of her wailing filled the room.

Eternity

Dr. Rahimullah was bent slightly forward at his desk with a posture which denoted anticipation. Opening a desk drawer he pulled out a pouch. "You know the oath we have been appointed to keep. Each of you must now place your ring in the pouch. I will then allow each of you to handle the physical contents of the pouch."

Dr. Dawud Malik, Ahmad as-Sirjani, Jamil al-Filisteeni, Khalid al-Misri, Dr. Abdullah Morgan, Dr. Bilal Stephens and Anwaar Zakaria stood. Dr. Rahimullah thought they had the appearance of the steeds of Allah. The men were well-chosen indeed.

One at a time, they dropped their rings into the pouch. Each of them said the same thing in a well-modulated voice, "I bear witness." Dr. Muhammad Rahimullah would rejoin, "That there is no god but Allah." The door was closed but should an individual have been present on the other side, it would have sounded like the strophe and antistrophe of a Greek chorus.

When all of the rings were in the pouch Dr. Rahimullah removed his own and placed it into the pouch. He then reached into a vest pocket to remove the ring of the murid. The silver band of this ring was a bit thicker. Inscribed on the inside of the band was one simple word. 'Arif

Dr. Rahimullah then moved to his wall safe and removed an object the size of a miniature Qur'an. The pages were protected by two covers made of silver and bound at the back with the hair of a black camel. The clasp on the front of the book was made of eighteen carat gold. Dangling from the clasp was a small ornamental key cast in silver and embedded with small gemstones. Carefully inscribed on the back of the key in script which was barely visible was one word. Qutb.

The silence in the room was as that of the time when the moon was cleft asunder in the valley of Makkah. Ahmad as-Sirjani sensed the emotional pulse in the room and quietly said, "The Hour of Judgment is nigh." The silence continued, heavy, now like the silence that follows the final groan of a pregnant woman before she gives birth. Khalid al-Misri cleared his throat tentatively. His eyes brimmed with tears. "I hardly have sufficient words to match my sentiment. To actually see, to actually touch what I have sworn on oath to protect with my last drop of blood, is beyond my wildest dreams." Dr. Abdullah Morgan echoed the sentiment. "I would cut out my own tongue before I would ever divulge the location of the treasure which is now before my very eyes." Dr. Dawud Malik allowed his eyes to sweep across the men and spoke in a firm voice. "It is as our Brother Muhammad Qutb told me in Jiddah. He had a dream while I was there. The pouch traveled to America." He said to me, "The Guardian of the pouch will continue to flee across the globe because of the Jews." The men shook their heads in agreement and looked knowingly at each other.

Dr. Rahimullah stood carefully with the prized possession and placed it in the hands of Khalid al-Misri. "You are the most senior in the Shura Council as my second in command. It will be for you to open the clasp and look at the pages first. We know that the pages were written by our Brother Sayyid Qutb. It was written immediately after he finished his first commentary for Fi Zilal al-Qur'an. His writing was considered so highly strategic that the work was placed under the guardianship of a special council selected to carry out his mandate and continue his work. Each of you seated here today are an extension of the vision of our Brother Qutb, because of the secrecy oath and your fidelity to duty. But for the mere satisfaction of the moment, let me rehearse the contents. The pages are fourteen in length. Each page represents one decade. Sayyid's guidance laid out the challenges of each decade for the forward movement of Islam in the West from the 1960's onward. What was unknown to each of us until today, what was only known to the Guardian, is the existence of the seven additional pages, each one a prayer. These prayers are for the years of the silent call; the three year windows our leadership takes every two decades to prepare the next generation for their task. When I read the prayers, my hands began to tremble. Surely today, we are under the shadow of a great man."

It was two a.m. when the men finally left the home of Dr. Rahimullah. Khalid al-Misri carried with him the pouch with the hair of the Prophet Muhammad. Dr. Dawud Malik carried the ring of the murid in a small silver box. Jamil al-Filisteeni had a large envelope in his hand. Across the back were wax seals bearing the imprint of the rings of each member of the Shura Council. In three days the men would make the flight on a private jet to return the work of Qutb to the land of his birth.

Dr. Rahimullah could not sleep. He wished that it were possible to also make the flight to Egypt. But there was much for him to do in the coming months. He must finish his work in America. And he must prepare for his return to Lebanon. He sat at his desk and contemplated the remarkable history of his own life. It was no less remarkable than the history of the Ummah over the centuries. There was no doubt in his mind and of one thing he was sure: that which Sayyid Qutb had prayed would come to pass in the future. So much of what he had written was already a present reality.

As the thin white line formed on the horizon Dr. Rahimullah placed his prayer rug on the floor in front of him. He heard his wife stirring in the bedroom. A good cup of tea would await him shortly. Smiling slightly, he bent down to straighten his prayer rug. And then, he was no more.

www.ingramcontent.com/pod-product-compliance
Lightning Source LLC
Chambersburg PA
CBHW051429170626
46809CB00006B/2388